REGRET

COMING HOME
BOOK 2

ALLYSON LINDT

Cover Design
DAQRI BERNARDO

ACELETTE PRESS

For my eternal dragon…

ONE

"I GET IT," LIZ SAID. THOUGH SHE WAS ON THE other end of the line, Jonathan heard the eye roll in her tone. "For the five millionth time—the world won't end if you can't answer your phone for a few hours at a time. Or a few days. I owe you for that debacle of a charity event. I'll handle things."

He scowled at the reminder, both of the disaster and that she wanted him to ignore work while he was on bereavement leave. "This doesn't make up for that, because you'll call me long before things get that bad." Every time he hit a bump in the dilapidated road, his rental car jolted, and he stuttered.

"Jonathan."

"*Liz.*" Even after ten years, the overgrowth here looked the same. There was no question which turnoff was the road to his destination. Trees overhung the driveway, their branches scraping the hood of the sedan. Weeds crept up through cracks in the asphalt, and bright splashes of purple, red, and blue blossoms peeked out from beyond the path.

She sighed. "Next time you ask for a favor, remind me you're uptight and incapable of delegation."

"Noted."

"Take care of things. Mourn your grandmother. Turn off your phone. Don't worry about the office until you're done." Her tone was sympathetic.

He smiled, despite the tension coursing through him at the idea of ignoring the office for so long. "Fine. But I'm not turning the phone off." He pulled up in front of the house. The white-painted wood was stark, as if it was touched up recently. More of the foliage dipped over the split-level home, dusting pollen and leaves onto the porch. A fist clenched around his chest at the rush of memories, and he swallowed it all back. Fortunately, a woman with distracting curves paced the porch running the front length of Nana's house, and gave him a new focus. Nosy neighbor? "I've got to go. Later," he said.

He disconnected without waiting for a reply from Liz. The woman didn't look back when he parked the car and shut off the engine. She poked at the rockers and the two-person swing, then turned her attention to the chain holding it up.

From behind, he could tell she was almost his height, with long legs, a narrow waist, and white-blonde hair piled in a messy bun on top her head.

Something tickled his memory, but he couldn't grasp it. He wasn't interested in digging too deep, in case it was associated with the summers he spent here. He climbed out of the car and strolled toward the house. "Excuse me. Can I help you?" he asked.

The woman spun to face him, and his stomach flipped. *Bailey.* The glasses perched on the edge of her nose didn't hide how clear her blue eyes were, or the smattering of freckles that smooshed up when she met his gaze and gave him a cool smile. She looked good.

"No." She closed the distance between them. "I think the time for that is long past, Mr. Wood-house." She rubbed her palms on faded jeans before extending one in greeting.

He shook her hand, using the couple-second pause to regain control of his senses. "People call me that every day, yet coming from you, it feels like you're talking to my father. Jonathan is fine."

"That's gonna be awkward, because I prefer you call me Ms. Moore." Her tone chilled him, despite the August sun trying to beat its way through his suit coat.

Something brushed against his leg and at the same time meowed, drawing his attention. A long-haired white cat wove itself around him. He gave the animal a half-smile. "Not now, pretty kitten." With every new pass of the cat, more fur decorated his dark slacks. "I'm not dressed for that."

Bailey bent at the waist, offering Jonathan a fantastic view down the front of her button-down top, and picked up the cat to scratch its head. "You're not really dressed for this, in general. Lucifer is helping you adjust your expectations. Aren't you, princess?" She looked at him again as she straightened and held up the cat.

"Truly kind of her." He reached out, keeping an arm's length between them, and teased behind the cat's ears for a few seconds, before shaking the fluff away and stepping aside as it drifted to the ground.

Bailey rolled her eyes. "Do you want me to get you gloves and a plastic slicker, sir?"

"I'm fine, thank you. I'm meeting with the person doing appraisal and handling Nana's estate sale, and then I'll be on my way. You and Lucifer can kick up dust and fur and laugh at me all you want once I'm gone." Jonathan wasn't sure what he'd done to incur the frigid reception, but he didn't plan on sticking around long enough for it to matter.

She set the cat down, and Lucifer strolled back to Jonathan's leg, hopped up on her back paws, propped the front against his shin, and mewled loudly.

"She's your grandmother's." Bailey winced. "Sorry. *Was.* I think she recognizes you."

He scooped Lucifer up—mostly to prove Baily wrong, and only partly to distract himself from another surge of grief—and held her close, scratching her chin. "See? A little fluff won't hurt me."

"Glad to hear it. I hope a little dust doesn't bother you either, because we've got a lot of cataloging to do. I'm the appraiser and auctioneer."

"Ah." He fumbled for a better response, but nothing offered itself. He wasn't used to being on his guard like this, even against an icy demeanor. So why did Bailey have him stunned silent? He shook the question aside. It was because being here reminded him how much he missed Nana. Nothing more.

Bailey was a part of the past, gnawing at his senses and insisting he give it attention. He'd push through it now, and cope when he got back to his hotel. "What do you need from me? I let you into the house, give you my number, and when you're done, you provide me with a list of what the estate holds and estimates?" Lucifer nipped his finger, and when he started, hopped from his arms and fled around the side of the house. What was he going to do with the cat? Someone local would give her a good home, right?

Bailey frowned. "Sure. We *can* do it that way.

Don't you want to see any of her belongings for yourself? It's my understanding the only items that go to auction are those you don't want. There are a lot of memories in there." She nodded at the house.

Exactly. Memories from spending every summer here, from childhood until he was eighteen. Of the ridiculous stories Nana convinced younger-him were true, about pirates and haunted beaches and hidden treasures. Of running away here when he was four-teen, only for his father to haul him back home a month later. Of watching Bailey celebrate her engagement to the biggest asshole on the island.

The past throbbed behind his temples. Nope. He wasn't interested in diving into any of that. Not with her here, not ever. He gave Bailey his widest smile. "No. I trust you. I'm not worried about value. I simply want her things to go to people who'll appreciate them." He handed her a business card. "Call me when you're done."

WHEN JONATHAN TURNED AWAY, Bailey clenched and loosened her fist several times, her arm hanging at her side. It took the last of her restraint to stay aloof with him, especially with how incredible he looked in that suit. Sandy-blond hair, cut so short it didn't brush his ears; navy jacket and slacks that accentu-ated broad shoulders, a defined chest, and long legs

—the bozo had to go and be more attractive than she remembered. That didn't stop her from pretending she didn't give a flying fig if he was the executor for this estate, any more than if anyone else were in his place.

But watching him turn his back on his heritage rubbed her wrong. "If Nana didn't want you to be a part of this, she would have left your name out of the will. Show some respect." The older woman's name was Nancy, but because she'd been like a grandmother to everyone on the island, they all called her Nana.

Jonathan shook his head. "I'll be in town for a few days," he called over his shoulder.

"You sure you can stand it here for that long?" She winced at the bitterness that tinged her question.

He dropped into the car. One leg stayed on the ground, propping the door open. "Don't have to. I'm staying on the mainland."

A gust shredded through the area, tearing at her hair. Dirt and debris bit into her face, and she closed her eyes against the gale. Through the howl, she heard a car engine start. When the weather ebbed enough for her to pry one eye open, she saw Jonathan backing out of the driveway.

"*Bozo.*" Her shout at the retreating vehicle vanished in the stiff wind. She turned back to the house, opened the door, and Luci shot past her legs to dart inside. This was for the best. The last thing Bailey needed was Jonathan hovering over her shoulder, sharing her personal space, and being... *him*.

She entered the house, locked everything behind her to keep it from rattling in the sudden gusts, and then paused. Where to start? Besides a little dust that had gathered in the last week, the home looked like Nana stepped out for the afternoon, instead of passing away. A bitter lump formed in Bailey's throat. She didn't understand how Jonathan could be so removed about the whole thing. Bailey wasn't even related to the woman, and she missed her terribly. Going through this place felt like she was disturbing ghosts.

She needed to get started, though. The kitchen was first. The fridge and freezer would need to be emptied. New, amazing, and disgusting smells wafted from the vegetable crisper. The stuff in the cupboards and pantry could go to the neighbors.

She headed upstairs next. Three rooms lined the hallway. The first on the left was an office. A desk and bookshelves to sift through. She wandered into the small room, running her fingers over worn spines without touching them. The assortment always amazed her—classic leather-bound tomes, mixed with scintillating romance novels. Women on the covers with barely covered, heaving chests, in the arms of their manly counterparts. This was where Bailey discovered how much she loved reading.

She blinked several times, to clear away the dust making her eyes water. Why wasn't Jonathan doing this? She left the room but couldn't bring herself to enter the other two. She knew what she'd find. On the left would be a twin bed, stripped of its sheets. Shelves, lined with model planes, dinosaurs, and plastic planets. All of it dusted, as if Nana expected teenage-Jonathan to return any day.

Nana's room was on the right. Bailey swallowed past a raw throat. Right. Time to see what was in the attic. Those memories shouldn't be attached to fresh, open wounds.

She reached the end of the hallway, found the rope dangling from the ceiling, and then tugged. The ladder to the attic scrolled down, feet landing near hers.

Sunlight streamed through the high windows and filtered through dust, greeting her as she climbed into the small space. Boxes, trunks, and crates lined the walls and spilled into the path like a broken Tetris game. She could do this. It was like any estate she worked with, it would take time, but she'd treat the things up here the way she always did —like precious parts of someone else's life, not her own.

She'd need an empty spot to shift things into. Enough space to rearrange as she went, so she could keep track of items to be auctioned versus those that held nothing but sentimental value. She grabbed the black marker and sticky notes from her back pocket, and started labeling in the corner that held the least. This was good. The methodical sorting would keep her mind off the tragedy that brought her here, and distract her from how irritated she was with Jonathan for shrugging this off as if it were a neighbor's vacation slides.

The first few boxes were easy. More books, all of them paperbacks. She sneezed several times, as she slid them toward their holding spot. Those would go up for auction in as-is sets.

She opened a trunk, to find uniform stacks of shoe boxes. Flipping the lid on the first revealed photos. Some had to be almost as old as Nana, in black and white, with yellowed edges and a girl in her late teens, posing with various people. They were mixed with others, in faded colors. A kid in a striped shirt and running shorts that barely covered his legs—Jonathan's father. Bailey ground her teeth. A stack of printed photos from an early-model photo printer sat at the bottom. A blonde girl with a bob that didn't reach her shoulders, on her skateboard next to a boy on a bike.

She crammed the photos back in their box, labeled the trunk *Personal*, and shoved it in the other direction. Someone else could finish sorting through them.

A loud pounding jarred her from her work. Someone hammering on the screen door. She tucked loose strands of hair behind her ears and made her way downstairs. A glance at the clock told her she'd been working for almost an hour and a half.

When she opened the door, she was shocked to see Jonathan standing on the other side. He'd shed the suit coat and tie, rolled his sleeves up, halfway to the elbow, and undone the top button on his shirt. "You're right." He gave her a cocky grin. "I should help."

She stared back in disbelief. "Really. Just like that, you changed your mind."

"That, and the bridge is closed because of a storm watch."

When tropical storms and hurricanes blew in, the roads between the Keys and mainland Florida flooded. It was common to shut down the bridges before that happened, rather than risk losing cars to floods or wind. Which meant he couldn't leave the island.

"How altruistic of you. Come on in." She unlocked the screen door and pushed the latch. The wind ripped the door from her hand, and Jonathan stepped back as it tore open and slammed against the side of the house.

TWO

FOR ABOUT HALF A SECOND, JONATHAN CONSIDERED bluffing about why he came back, and clinging to the *I changed my mind excuse*. Bailey would figure out the reality soon, and he'd get shit for it either way. Might as well stick with the truth, mixed with light teasing, and try to gloss things over quickly.

He wasn't prepared for how she looked when she greeted him. His hand twitched by his side, and he held back the desire to reach up and brush away the smudges of dirt on her cheeks or trace away the tear tracks. He stepped around her. "Thanks." Now that he'd had time to think, the clouds were gone from his mind, and he could slide into the routine he was used to. "I didn't expect them to upgrade the storm so fast." The forecast when he came out here put the tropical storm below Category 1 and predicted it sliding around the peninsula. It might, still. Closing the roads was a precaution. Even if the rain hit, he'd be out of here by morning.

Stepping into the house sent a fresh wave of memories over him, stronger than the gusts outside. Every sight knocked an old image loose, from the orange shag throw-rug covering hardwood in the living room, to the brown couch with a crocheted blanket on the back, to the off-balance wooden entertainment center that shouldn't have stood for two days, let alone two decades. The power of everything almost made him stumble.

Bailey barely gave him a glance before heading toward the stairs. "If you're staying here, you'll want to clean out the fridge. Probably call Greg's Market and have them drop off some milk, unless you drink your coffee black."

"I'm sure I'll be fine." If she wanted him in the kitchen where she wouldn't be, that meant no small talk. Given the ice still rolling from her, that was fine, and cleaning out the fridge should be disgusting enough to keep his mind occupied.

The cat looked at him from her perch on the dining room table, yawned, and then settled back down to sleep. *Spoiled ball of fluff.* He was amused at the disdain, rather than irritated. He picked her up, and she whined in protest. "Sorry, princess. Not on the table."

He set her on the ground, and she looked up at him for a moment before hopping back up.

"No." He forced himself to sound sterner. He moved her again, and she returned to her resting spot as quickly.

"She's more welcome up there than you are," Bailey called.

"I'm not trying to sit on the table."

"You know what I mean." She poked her head around the corner, her scowl telling him she didn't find the comment as funny as he did.

"Come on." He gave her the smile that smoothed over most sticky situations. "I'm back, aren't I?"

"About that— Let's not gloss over the fact that you don't want to be here. The barricade that closes off the bridge back to the mainland is twenty minutes away. Half an hour, in the worst weather. Why did it take you almost an hour and a half to return?"

Because he spent forty-five minutes trying to convince himself they might open things up if he waited. "I had to make a couple of calls."

"Of course. Don't let me keep you from the important work." Sarcasm coated her words. "You know where everything is. Nothing's moved in at least twenty years. I'll be upstairs."

"You don't have to do this now. Take the night off. Come back when I'm not here." So maybe he couldn't do playful and kind. Regardless of his approach, he seemed to rub her the wrong way.

She made a noise that was half-sigh, half-growl, and planted herself in front of him, lips pursed. "Have you ever managed an estate sale?"

"No."

"Then I'll fill in some of the blanks for you. I have a limited number of days to go through everything in this house, cellar to roof, and figure out what can be sold—along with their opening bids—and what needs to be donated, or set aside for you to not deal with. I don't get to take time off, because regardless of what you think, the work is going to take more than a couple of hours and making *a list of stuff.*"

He pinched the bridge of his nose. "All right. I want to get this out of the way as quickly and smoothly as I'm sure you do. So, what's your problem with me?"

She gave a bitter laugh, choked it off, and then laughed again. "*Wow.* Where to start? Okay. Let's assume you want the quick and compact answer. You're not even freaking mourning. That woman loved you more than anything. You can't fathom how often she talked about you—how well you were doing; how proud she was of you. Then you don't have the balls to come to her wake. You drive up two days later, as if being here is an inconvenience for you, toss me a phone number, and head back to work."

"First of all, I *was* at her wake. I couldn't stay. I

wanted to." He refused to stall on the words, despite the acid surging up his throat. "I was at her service, and I was at the beach when her ashes were scattered, and—God help me—I'm grateful she asked for someone else to do that." He wouldn't sink into the grief tightening around his heart and lungs, making it hard to breathe. At both affairs, he'd left before many people saw him. The few handshakes and obligatory condolences were enough to drill into his core.

At least his father wasn't there. Not that Jonathan was surprised. The only time his old man had spoken to him in the last five years, was a bitter email a week ago that said, *Congratulations on your inheritance.* Nana left Dad out of the will. Jonathan had fought off the sadness off this long. Giving in now didn't help anyone. "You have less than zero idea how much this hurts."

"Is that so? You've got an exclusive on grief now? Is it something you picked up as part of a discount investment portfolio? She might have been *your* grandmother, but she was here for me when no one else was." She worked her jaw up and down, as if she wanted to say more, but then clamped her mouth shut.

Like I should have been. The unwelcome thought taunted him. What was he supposed to do for Bailey? She turned him down last time he offered his help. Made it clear that was the last thing she wanted. "Then you must have some idea how much it hurts that I didn't get to say *goodbye* to her."

"That was your choice. If you hadn't cut us all out of your life—"

"What?" Something inside snapped, and he let anger replace guilt. "All the letters exchanged. Photos, post cards, email she and I sent back and forth—don't accuse me of cutting and running because I wasn't talking to *you*. She never gave me any hint something was wrong. I couldn't have known."

"That's a nice excuse. Nothing stopped you from coming back, before then."

"*Everything* stopped me from coming back." Fuck. He didn't mean to say that. Didn't want her to know it took years, to get over the last fight he and Bailey had. Longer to convince himself what happened to her after wasn't his fault. At least he never questioned that getting over her was the right decision. Leaving this place behind was one of his best calls, and as soon as this estate deal was over, he'd do it again.

BAILEY KNEW she was being cruel. Sometime in the last few minutes, this argument stopped being about Nana and started being about her, and that was self-ish. Red rimmed Jonathan's eyes, and his voice cracked each time it rose to a shout. He kept in touch with Nana, and Bailey had no idea? Still, she couldn't back off. She didn't know where her misery ended and her spite began. "Fine. You had your reasons. Sorry for questioning you." She couldn't even force that to sound genuine. "I need to get back to work."

She really needed to get to the bathroom, lock the door, and let the tears stream down her face until she was spent. Then, after she washed that away, she could return to her sorting.

"Bailey." He grabbed her arm.

She couldn't find the energy to wrench away. "Let go."

He moved to stand in front of her, then dropped his grip, setting his palm on her face and forcing her gaze to his. "I'm sorry." The anguish in his words was reflected in the brown depths of his eyes. "I'm sorry she's gone. I'm sorry it hurts. I wish more than anything that she were still here."

Something in his tone snapped the dam inside her, and she sobbed so hard it rocked through her frame and ached in her joints.

"Damn it," he said, as he gathered her in his arms.

She didn't have the will to struggle. Instead, she buried her face against his chest, and gripped his shirt as if it could keep her from shattering into a million pieces. A tiny voice in her head nagged that she needed to pull herself together. There was no way she could listen. The crying wouldn't stop. Even when he rested his forehead against the top of her skull and muttered random things like *I get it* and *me too*.

She cried until his shirt was wetter than her cheeks. Until the sobs became whimpers and then faded to sniffles. She must be a freaking mess right now. Did she care?

"I'm making you take the night off." His chin moved against her head when he spoke, his words vibrating through her.

"You're not the boss of me." The childish retort scraped through her raw throat.

He gave a weak laugh. "Technically, I am. Executor of the estate, right? I say you're done for today."

"Yes, sir." She didn't want to pull away. The comfort was nice. Besides, she cared at least a little about how red and puffy her face was.

He squeezed her tight, and then relaxed his arms.

She backed away, not meeting his gaze. "I'll be back," she said and headed for the bathroom upstairs.

She locked the door behind her and let the cold water run over her hands and wrists until her skin was numb. After she splashed her face, she didn't dare look in the mirror for several minutes.

Agony stared back from her reflection, but her face was mostly clear. Her insides felt like sandpaper, but the empty pit in her gut didn't gape as wide as it had over the last week. Her mind tried to analyze what just happened, and revolted when it hit a blank wall that refused to budge. That was okay with her. She'd process later, when she was home alone with the cold beer waiting in her fridge.

She refastened her hair in a ponytail, dried her skin, and made her way downstairs. Jonathan sat at the kitchen table, as far from Luci as possible, two glasses in front of him. He'd given up trying to move the cat. Bailey did a double take when she saw he wore a white T-shirt, and slacks. His button-down was draped over the back of another chair. She wasn't going to stare at the way the cotton stretched over his chest, highlighting the definition every time he shifted.

To distract herself, she picked up the discarded shirt. She winced when she saw the dust and moisture streaking the front. "I'm sorry."

He shrugged. "It'll wash out. If not, it's replaceable. I called Greg's. They're delivering milk and deli sandwiches."

"I really can't stay." Or didn't think it was a good idea. Or both.

He nodded at the amber liquid over ice. "You were going to be here for a few more hours anyway.

At least have a drink with me." He nudged a glass in her direction.

Luci moved to sniff the contents, then hopped from the table and strolled into the other room.

"That's either a good sign or a really bad one." Bailey's desire to argue had evaporated. She took a sip and let the sweet, smooth flavor burn down her throat. The familiar taste of ginger ale and whiskey tugged at her grief again, but she was too spent to fall into it. "Ale and Jack."

He shrugged, then took a swig of his own drink. "It was what I could find the mixings for."

When he ran away from home and came here, she'd been thrilled. It meant unexpected extra time with her best friend. They raided her parents' pantry when Mom and Dad were out one evening, and stuffed themselves on cheese puffs and booze. It only took a can of soda and a couple shots of Jack Daniels, before they were giggling and falling over each other. Rather than ground her, her parents decided to go the humiliation route and told the entire town what a lightweight she was. Everyone called them Ale and Jack for the rest of their teenage years.

"It's perfect." She finished her drink.

"You're staying at least until after dinner."

The bitterness and her desire to fight back were gone. She found the cold cans of soda on the counter next to the fridge, along with the liquor.

Grabbing both, she crossed the room back to the table, and dropped into a chair next to Jonathan. She poured them each another drink, before replying, "Only if we get the wake you chickened out on."

"I didn't chicken out."

"Whatever." She stared back, hoping her skepticism showed on her face.

He clinked his glass to hers. "To Nana."

"To Nana." She downed half her drink in a single swallow. A pleasant haze filled her head, fuzzing some of the rough edges. Maybe for tonight, she could block out the loss.

THREE

Jᴏɴᴀᴛʜᴀɴ ᴅɪᴅɴ'ᴛ ꜱʟᴀᴍ ᴛʜᴇ ꜱᴇᴄᴏɴᴅ ᴅʀɪɴᴋ ᴀꜱ quickly as the first, and by number three, he was willing to nurse it. The liquor seeped into the cracks of sympathy that formed when Bailey broke down, and helped him find his balance again.

The wind howled through the trees. Small branches banged into the building, but no rain fell. As long as the gusts died by morning, he'd be back to his hotel, catching up on work, and riding out this auction thing from a location where the roads didn't randomly close and he didn't have to worry about being caught in a hurricane.

He watched Bailey watch her cup. What was he supposed to say?

"She was really proud of you." Bailey broke the silence first. "Bragged to everyone who would listen about how brilliant and successful her grandson was."

He took another swallow of his drink and let it warm his face and throat.

She clinked the ice inside her glass. "She only had one fear for you—she was terrified you'd turn out like your dad."

"A humorless fuck, who let his ego drive him into failure and shut down because he made a mistake?"

"At least the two of you are as close as ever." Bailey's laugh was sarcastic. "But no. She was worried you spent too much time working. That you'd lose track of life and the things you enjoyed."

"What I enjoy is the job I built for myself. I'm fucking incredible at it, and I've always known it takes long hours. I don't have a problem with that."

"Which is why your phone is on the table next to you. I was gone for... ten minutes? Fifteen? Did it give you time to check in? Sorry. I didn't mean to be snippy."

This wasn't pleasant reminiscing about the good things, and he wanted to enhance the buzz of liquor, not destroy it. "What about you?" He kept his tone curious and kind. "Appraisal and auction is specialized work. Not quite Indiana Jones, but I see the parallels." When she was younger, she wanted to be a world-renowned archaeological adventurer.

He missed the fun they had when they were

teenagers. The thought hit him hard. Not just the wild, unattainable dreams, but the friendship. Would they ever be able to find that again? The question came from left field, but he liked the sound of it. This felt like a good start, but it was rocky. Every other sentence, he misstepped.

"No, it's not the same. But I see more variety in the antiques than your standard archaeologist, and there's a lot less risk of me breaking something before it's completely unearthed."

"I bet you're amazing at what you do." This was better. He liked the way a smile lingered on her face.

She tugged on her ponytail, a sparkle dancing in her eyes. "I like to think I'm good at spotting both the valuable antiques and the things that have senti-mental value—the art that fills people's hearts with passion. I..." She bit the inside of her cheek. "Yeah."

Curious. "What aren't you saying?"

"So much more than we have time for tonight." She knocked back the rest of her drink. "That's a big question."

"I'll be more specific. What aren't you saying about the art?"

"It's silly."

There was a crash outside, and they both jumped. Gusts whistled against the wood siding. She laughed and shook her head. "You'd think I'd be used to the thunder and other sounds by now.

Gets me every time. Probably for the rest of my life."

"I promise not to laugh." He didn't want to lose this thread of conversation. "You've always wanted to discover the rare and the beautiful and share them with the world. Is that what your job is about?"

"It's exactly that, and not at all in the way you'd think." She fiddled with the whiskey bottle but didn't pour another shot.

Silence stretched between them, spanning seconds and then minutes. He didn't want to jar her from wherever she had drifted to.

She shook her head and looked at him. "I want to uncover new talent, not antiques. There's a gallery on Main Street. I help move some of their pieces when I can. The owner is sweet—I adore her —but she's selling the place, to move to North Carolina and take care of her father, rather than put him in a nursing home. I know it's whimsical, but I wish I could buy it. Fill it with talent from everywhere."

"It's a lovely dream. You know places like that rarely make much money."

She scowled at him. "Not everything is about the cash flow."

"An investment like buying an art gallery is." He didn't want to offend her, but the thought of her wasting her time on a venture that would leave her broke... How could he explain his concern?

The doorbell rang, saving him from having to push the harsh truth. He stood faster than he intended, and his chair screeched across the Spanish tile. He cringed. "That's probably Greg's. Be right back."

Bailey's frustrated and wounded expression drilled into his mind, as he made his way into the living room and answered the door. The kid outside winced against the wind and thrust a paper bag at Jonathan as soon as the opening was wide enough. "Eight sixty-two," the teenager said.

Jonathan glanced at the delivery and set it aside. "For milk and two sandwiches?"

"Yes. Eight sixty-two."

Cheap food. One thing to love about the small-town feel. Jonathan pulled a twenty from his wallet and handed it over. "Keep the change."

"Thanks, man." The boy's smile made it look as if the tip was worth braving the storm for. He bolted back to the rusted hatchback parked next to Jonathan's rental.

Jonathan was about to turn back inside, when a ball of white fluff darted between his legs, shot across the porch, and disappeared around the side of the house. "*Lucifer.*" The wind swallowed his shout. Though it was barely seven in the evening, the clouds swallowed the sun, making it look like the sun had set.

"What happened?" Bailey asked.

He whirled to face her. "Cat ran outside." He hissed as he looked at the raging weather. "I'm going to go find her."

"Wait." Bailey vanished into the kitchen. Things rattled. Drawers and cabinet doors opened and closed. A moment later, she returned with a flashlight in one hand and a bag of—Jonathan squinted—cat treats in the other. She handed him the flashlight. "Let's go."

He secured the front door behind her, then shone the light on the ground, following the path he saw the animal take. "Don't suppose you know if she has a favorite hiding place?"

"Under the rose bushes around back. C'mon, pretty Luci." She rattled the treat bag and called out every few seconds, as she walked next to Jonathan.

As Bailey predicted, Lucifer waited behind the house, cowering under a bush. Her ears were pressed back against her head, eyes wide and body flat against the ground. She didn't come when called, but she also didn't run.

"Come on, sweetheart." Jonathan crouched low and approached her slowly, hand outstretched. The cat relaxed and twitched her nose. "That's right." He handed the flashlight to Bailey, and then dropped to his knees. Maybe he was going to too much trouble for a fucking cat, but he couldn't leave her outside in this kind of weather. He got close enough to touch her and let her sniff his fingers. Perfect. With a twist, he grabbed for the scruff of her neck.

She jerked out of his grasp and bolted again.

"God damn it." He rocked back onto his heels with a frustrated sigh, trying to ignore the mud staining his slacks.

THE SHARP WIND was stealing Bailey's buzz almost as quickly as Jonathan's disdain did, when she told him about her dream. Fortunately, the Jack lingered in her veins and chased away the chill, and once they got back inside, another shot or two would numb the sting of the interrupted conversation. She didn't know whether to tease him or offer sympathy for his dirt streaked clothing. He was searching for Luci though, and that earned him several stars in the *maybe some of my friend is still in there* column in her mind.

A door slammed into stone, and then rattled back and forth, causing her to squeal and jump. She covered her mouth, embarrassed at the reaction.

"Cellar?" Jonathan asked.

"Probably."

"What are the odds the cat's down there?"

"Depends on if this is a coincidence, or the gods just want to make me squirm." She gave him a nervous smile. The house had an outdoor cellar that had given her the creeps for as long as she could remember. She and Jonathan followed the cement steps down to the wooden door that rattled in the wind. Beyond that lay stone walls and wooden shelves. Once upon a time, they were full of canned goods the local people gave Nana as thank-you gifts for various things. Over the last few years, she'd worked to get rid of most of the stock and empty the room.

Bailey swung the beam of the flashlight, and it caught the shelves, casting tall shadows on the far wall. "Yup. Still freaking creepy."

"I'll keep you safe," Jonathan said in an artificially loud baritone. "As long as there are no spiders." He rested a hand at the small of her back and nudged her forward. The warmth of his palm seared through her shirt and calmed her more than she wanted.

A hiss drew her attention, and she pointed the light toward the sound. Luci crouched on the top of a shelf, a few feet away, next to a bowl. "Come here, princess," Bailey cooed.

The cat flattened her ears and bared her teeth, then leapt. Her tail caught the bowl, sending it tumbling down on top of Jonathan and soaking him with rancid water. Luci landed on Bailey's shoulder and allowed herself to be cradled.

"Fucking hell." Jonathan grimaced and shook away the foul-smelling liquid.

This time Bailey couldn't hide her laugh. "I'm sorry." She sounded anything but. "I shouldn't."

He gave her a sheepish grin. "You should. And *we* should get back inside, so I can rinse this off. Ugh."

The moment they were in the house, Lucifer hopped from Bailey's arms and disappeared somewhere in the house. Bailey took the opportunity to survey the true damage. Jonathan's hair held a green tinge in places and was plastered to his head. His shirt was half drenched. Mud and slime caked his slacks. But at least he'd stopped dripping between the cellar and here.

"You know what sucks the most about this?" he asked.

She shook her head, another bout of giggles threatening to burst out of her.

"My luggage is back at the hotel. If I were at home, at least I'd have a gym bag in the car."

She was tempted to tell him he was welcome to roam the house naked, but she needed more liquor in her system for that. "Go take a shower, leave your stuff outside the bathroom, and I'll toss whatever's not dry-clean only in the wash. I'll find you a bathrobe or sweats or something."

"Nana was six inches shorter than me."

"I'm sure one of her guests left clothing here. Or I can run back into town and grab you some shorts and a T-shirt from a gift shop."

He twisted his mouth, as if he didn't agree. After a few seconds hesitation, he turned toward the stairs. "We both know nothing's open here after eight, except the diner. If you find me clothes here, I'll be eternally grateful."

She grabbed his clothes when he handed them through the bathroom door, tossed them in the washing machine, then went in search of something for him to wear. After a lot of digging, she found a couple of long nightgowns, a satin robe that was meant to reach mid-thigh, and a couple pairs of terrycloth shorts. She'd let him make the decision.

"Bailey?" His voice carried down the corridor. "Clothes?"

She set the stack in the hand he stretched out through the crack in the bathroom door. He closed the door, and seconds later she heard, "Are you fucking kidding me?"

"I couldn't find anything else."

"Figures. Give me a few minutes, and I'll be out."

While she waited, she put away the milk— someone really needed to clean that fridge—set the sandwiches out on plates, and poured them each another drink. Hinges creaked behind her. She set down the bottle of Jack and turned, curious to see which option he went with and prepared to stifle a laugh.

The footsteps on the second floor moved away from her, and she frowned. Silence settled in. Should she call out? He probably wanted to see what he could scrounge for himself. Before she could decide what to do next, the stairs creaked. Seconds later, he stepped into the dining room doorway, a paisley sheet wrapped around him like a toga.

He leaned against the wall, the position elongating his frame, and wiggled his eyebrows. "You think I can start a new fashion trend?"

"If your target audience is frat boys. Speaking of —I don't think I've ever seen someone actually wear a sheet-toga. Where did you learn that?"

"I was a frat boy. Shall we?" He nodded at the food.

They settled at the table and ate in silence. She wasn't sure what to say. On the one hand, she'd love to find that pleasant balance of fun and banter they used to have. That same feeling that peeked its head up a few times this afternoon. She didn't want to hit one of those snags, where something set either him or her off, though. "I wonder why Nana never mentioned you still wrote to her." She hid her wince. That was anything but a neutral topic.

He met her gaze for a moment, expression flat.

He'd always had a brutal poker face. "Maybe she assumed it was a given."

"You said mail. Like handwritten letters and such?" Why was she pushing this?

"With real stamps and real ink and real paper."

"Hmm." Bailey couldn't come up with anything better.

Jonathan studied her. "I'm sorry about what happened with Danny."

The name curdled in her gut, and she set her food aside in favor of another drink. "How much do you know?" Betrayal gnawed at her. She'd asked Nana to keep the details private. The entire town knew about the divorce, but Bailey couldn't stand the thought of the whispers she'd hear if they knew why. It was worse with Jonathan, though. He'd tried to warn her. Pleaded with her not to marry the asshole. And she told him he was jealous.

But he'd been right. The cheating would have been enough, but there was so much more to it than he guessed. The verbal abuse. The way Danny made her doubt herself. His suicide threats. The bankruptcy she was still paying for... The one thing she could thank her ex for was she knew better than to get involved now. Flings on the mainland were easy—no heartbreak, no having to see their faces the morning after. The way life should be.

"Not a lot. Just that it ended badly and you were coping," Jonathan said.

The reality pushed at her lips, wanting to spill out, but she washed it down with another drink. This wasn't the night for confessions. "Exactly. And thank you." She braced herself for more questions. Or pity. Or at least an *I told you so*.

"She never mentioned Lucifer." He didn't flinch, as he slid to a new topic.

Gratitude spilled through Bailey. "Luci's only been here about six months. Showed up on the porch one day. Maybe a tourist left her behind; we don't know. But she pretty much invited herself in and never left. What have you been up to? Nana bragged a lot, but never gave more details than you're a big, important executive for *some technology something or other*." Bailey also knew he paid his way through college with day-trading investments. Even as a teenager, he had a scary-good knack for buying and selling at the right time. An eye for numbers, trends, and how business decisions impacted both. He refused to go into brokerage though, because he wouldn't follow in his father's footsteps.

"Well"—he refilled both their glasses—"I was, until about six months ago. I've got a handful of partners now, and we invest in businesses that might not find funding elsewhere."

Angel investors. That sounded almost selfless and sweet. The whiskey drilled into her head, making everything a little more sparkly. "Do you keep in touch with the rest of your family?"

"You know I don't. But this evening isn't about me. You said Nana was there for you when no one else was. I understand it went both ways. Thank you for that."

She ducked her head, not sure if the heat scorching her cheeks was embarrassment for the recognition, or because of the drinking. His comment from earlier, about Nana never hinting something was wrong, rushed back. "She wasn't sick, you know. She had the normal aches and pains that come with age, but nothing else. There was nothing you could have done for her, even if you were here."

When he smiled, lines of tension vanished from his forehead. He really was sexy, ridiculous sheet not-withstanding. If they didn't have the shared past —if he were a random stranger, instead of her childhood friend—she'd consider hooking up for the night. Then again, he'd be gone as soon as the roads opened. What made him any less temporary than the next guy? Lingering traces of his warm touch teased her. The comfort when he held her. The power in his grip.

They ate and drank and glossed over the details of their lives since they last saw each other. By the time they moved to the living room, the bottle of Jack was almost empty. A pleasant haze clouded her thoughts, and every other thing either of them said made her giggle.

He settled on the couch. "Is the storm clearing up enough for me to escort you home?"

"You're not driving." She took the spot next to him.

"I'll walk you there, then."

She straddled his legs and wrapped her arms around his neck. A tiny voice in the back of her head asked what she was doing, but the whiskey and the wind drowned it out. "You're such a gentleman," she said.

He rested a hand at the back of her neck, holding her head, and searched her eyes. "What are you doing?"

"Not thinking." She crashed her mouth down on his. When he didn't respond, ice filled her veins, but then he tightened his grip, and kissed back hard and hungrily.

This might be the biggest mistake she'd made… On second thought, nothing could top the disaster that was her marriage, and God, he felt good beneath her.

FOUR

A TINY ANNOYING VOICE BUZZED IN THE BACK OF Jonathan's mind. *This is a bad idea.* It wasn't enough to make him stop. With only a sheet between him and Bailey, her every shift ground into him, sending desire racing across his skin. She whimpered and dug her fingers into his chest. Whiskey and ginger ale flooded his senses and danced with their tongues.

She's drunk.

I don't do one-night stands.

I'll never see her again after this week.

I wanted my friend back. This isn't the way to go about it.

Fucking logic. Fortunately, he was drunk too, which made it easier to ignore everything but the warm weight pressing into his cock, tempting him.

"The Jack was a brilliant find," she said, and

tilted her head back with a sigh when he drew his lips down her throat. "Best way to remove our reservations." Her words tugged harder at the protests in his head.

It didn't make him pull away. He kissed along her jaw, up to her ear. "Until we wake up tomorrow."

"Doesn't matter. You're leaving as soon as the roads open. It's not like you'll have to look me in the eye ever again." The lust and teasing in her voice didn't cover the disdain. She ducked her head. "I didn't mean... I don't know."

He pulled back as far as was possible, with her still in his lap, and watched her, unsure if he was grateful or disappointed that she wouldn't meet his gaze. The dryer buzzed, making them both jump but not shredding the blanket of tension filling the room. He moved his hands to her hips, shifted her aside, and untangled himself enough to stand. "I'm going to grab at least another layer of clothing. Then we'll talk."

"I'd rather not." She flopped back on the couch like a rag doll, gaze pointed at the ceiling.

"I'll be back in less than two minutes. Promise you won't to do something stupid, like head out into that storm to avoid me."

"I promise."

Jonathan headed to the laundry room. His boxers and T-shirt weren't much better than the sheet, especially if he couldn't keep his dick from poking out. Bailey's words killed his arousal though, and as long as he kept his mind on that instead of the moments leading up to it, he'd be fine. If he grabbed a throw and draped it over his lap, while sitting as far from her as possible and still staying in the same room, that would help too.

He took a little more time to wrap his thoughts in resolution, then returned to the living room. Bailey was curled up on the couch, breathing steadily, her eyes closed. He approached with hesitation. She didn't stir. *Figures.*

He was grateful for the reprieve. He brushed a strand of hair from her face, and she batted away his hand but never opened her eyes. This was better. They could talk in the morning, with cooler heads. He tugged the crocheted afghan from the back of the sofa and draped it over her, then made himself comfortable in the recliner across from her.

Sleep wouldn't come. He stared at the clock on the far wall, watching minutes tick away. The click of the second hand drilled into his jumbled thoughts. Now he remembered why he didn't drink. There was no order in his head when he let things get out of control. The patterns vanished, and he couldn't find structure.

A growl tore through him. He pushed from the chair and wandered to the bookshelf, to find something to read until his mind shut up and let him sleep. He traced the bindings with his fingers, but instead of grabbing one of the novels, he plucked a photo album from the shelf.

He settled back into the chair and flipped open to a random page. He wasn't sure when the faded photos were taken, until he turned to one of himself at five. Shaggy hair, horrible khaki shorts. He turned to another set. Nana wasn't in any of them. She kept the photos of her in boxes in the attic. Said she already remembered herself; she wanted memories of the people around her instead. The book was filled with photos of families, houses, local stores, pets, and so much more.

It gnawed at his chest, while dust and loose flakes of dried adhesive stung his eyes until his vision blurred. Bailey said no one saw Nana's death coming. Jonathan didn't believe that. Someone must have known. Healthy people didn't just pass away in the middle of the night. She took care of everyone in this fucking town, and she still died without—

He shoved the thought aside but couldn't bury the grief anymore. It mingled with bitterness. Guilt, that he was as responsible as anyone. An empty pit that threatened to devour him from the inside out.

JONATHAN'S FACE WAS HOT, and his eyes ached. He pried them open, and then clenched them shut again when the sunlight jammed into his vision. The rest of his senses prickled his consciousness. A jab in his neck, from falling asleep in the chair. A rancid taste coating his tongue. The alluring scent of fresh coffee. The clock said it was almost nine. He hadn't slept that late in... he didn't know how long.

As he forced himself to sit and stretch, he realized the couch was empty. He strained his ears, but didn't hear movement anywhere in the house. Last night's wind had died down, so it didn't interfere. The awkward scene with Bailey rushed back, as well as his looking through pictures after. He rubbed his eyes, to drive away more of the discomfort, stood, and put the album back its place on the shelf.

"Bailey?" he called out. No answer. Maybe she was in the attic, but he'd hear her overhead in that case.

He wandered into the kitchen and found note on the table, scrawled in familiar block-letter handwriting.

I'm sorry about last night. I have to check off some to-dos this morning. Be back at noon. Hope you'll stick around. We can have that talk. - Bailey

PS - coffee's fresh.

The conversation still needed to happen, but a little time to recover from his hangover and change into something that covered him a little more was a good thing. Coffee first. He opened the fridge, to grab the milk, and the stench threatened to evict the contents of his stomach.

Coffee second. He grabbed a couple of trash bags and proceeded to throw away everything but the milk, then deposited the garbage in the can by the side of the house.

By the time he finished his work and had a little caffeine running through his system, it was almost ten. Still plenty of time to get back to the hotel, change, and return before Bailey. He left her a note in return, saying he went to get fresh clothes and would be back, then pulled on his slacks, cringing at the dirt that flaked off and the stiff legs. When he reached the front door, Lucifer tried to dart between his legs, but this time Jonathan was ready. He kept her at bay, and managed to maneuver her inside and still step outside. "Stay," he said.

She yawned and sauntered toward the stairs. As he locked up, he made a mental note to ask Bailey who he could hand the cat over to. Then he was on his way back to the mainland.

BAILEY WOKE up to Jonathan in the chair and a cat sleeping on her hip. The asinine things she said the night before slammed into her skull like a mallet. What the freak was wrong with her? She was surprised Jonathan stuck around, after what she did. Not that he had a lot of choice.

She owed him so many apologies. And her gratitude for him being sensible when she wasn't. He was the friend she remembered, and she almost destroyed that because... Why? What had she been thinking? That was the one answer not coming to her.

Her morning tasks—things she couldn't put off—needed attention, but she itched to stay here and make things right. *Screw it.* She hoped he'd still be here when she got back, but wouldn't blame him for walking away as soon as the roads let him. She set up the coffee, left him a note, and then walked the half mile or so down the beach, to her own cottage. An hour later, showered and dressed, she drove into town.

Main Street on the small island was lined with wood-faced shops painted in bright colors. In the summer, they got tourists who skipped the more popular Keys in favor of that small-town feeling, but in early October, mostly locals strolled on the brick walkways. Bailey made a quick stop at the bank, for a cashier's check. Most of the clients she acted as an agent for were fine with digital transactions, but her next stop only dealt in paper. Said the money didn't feel real when it was numbers flowing from one screen to another.

Bailey smiled and waved at the handful of

people she passed between the bank and the art gallery near the end of the block. The decor inside was a subtle array of beige and taupe. Photos and paintings decorated the walls. Pedestals and easels dotted the floor, displaying sculpture and pottery.

"I'll be right down." Margaret's voice carried from the loft above.

Bailey followed the call to the open second floor and found the older woman sifting through a series of canvases stacked against the far wall. "Pay day."

Margaret jumped and whirled, her hand flying to her chest. "Don't sneak up on me."

"It's more fun this way," Bailey said in a teasing voice. "I found buyers for the silver and the two mirrors. I've got your money." Because of her connections with various auction houses, she helped the people around town move valuables from time to time. Margaret was slowly getting rid of everything she didn't think would move well with her to North Carolina.

"Come to the counter." Margaret led the way downstairs.

Bailey handed over the cashier's check when they reached their destination. Margaret examined it and furrowed her brow. "Did you take your share?"

"Of course." Bailey didn't hesitate to lie. She was supposed to keep a commission, but the older woman needed this money. Margaret was about to take on a huge expense, and when she was tired or having an off day, she tended to let slip how much the move was really going to cost her. Bailey made enough off her other dealings; she could afford to take a hit here and there.

"Are you sure? What kind of total minus fifteen percent equals exactly three-thousand dollars? Isn't that an odd coincidence?"

"I suppose." Bailey laughed, not having an excuse for the round figure. Maybe she should have thought of that and had the bank throw on a couple odd numbers at the end. "Anyway. I need to run. Working on cataloging Nana's place."

A shadow passed over Margaret's face. "Of course. How are you holding up?"

"Fine." This time the deception was more difficult.

"If you're sure. But stop by if you need an ear."

"Thanks." Bailey wasn't doing that. They exchanged a few more *goodbyes*, and she was gone again. She made a couple more stops in town, but her mind was already wandering to what waited for her. Not only the conversation with Jonathan, but the trip into the past. It was harder to force her smile in the grocery store and post office, and by the time she returned to Nana's, she felt drained.

Jonathan's car wasn't there, but a couple new trash bags sat outside. He cleaned out the fridge. That brought a little smile to her lips.

Inside, she found a note from him on top of hers. He'd gone to his hotel to change, but he wanted to talk too. He promised to be back before she was. She glanced at the clock on her phone. Twelve-fifteen. Something must have held him up.

She stashed the groceries in the fridge, then threw together a couple of sandwiches for lunch, and set them to chill as well.

Should she start working, and risk not hearing him come in, or wait a little longer?

A knock answered the question for her. "It's your house," she called. "You can just walk in…" She trailed off when she opened the door and found a couple on the front porch instead of Jonathan. "Can I help you?" she asked.

"I'm looking for Nancy?" the man said.

Bailey's grief slid back in. Not the steal-her-breath mourning she felt yesterday, but a gray cloud that mocked her. "Are you friends of the family?" She was pretty sure they weren't, but didn't know what else to ask.

He intertwined his fingers with the woman next to him. They were probably five or so years older than Bailey, and the way they stood near each other radiated affection. "Yes, and no. We vacationed here a few years ago. Separately. She introduced us, and we've been together since. We finally made it back this way and wanted to stop by and thank her."

"She passed away about a week ago." The

words filled Bailey with pain. Nana was responsible for a lot of hookups in town, involving both locals and tourists. That was another thing to miss now she was gone.

"Oh." The woman's face fell. "We didn't realize. I— I'm sorry."

"Thank you. Since you're here, would you like to come in? I'd love to hear about how you met." That was the polite thing to say.

The man shook his head. "Thank you, but we can't intrude on your mourning. Again, our sympathies."

"Thanks." Bailey let the door drift shut, as they walked back to their car. The longer she stood there, the more heavily sadness weighed on her. She needed something to take her mind off this. *Work.* Sifting through those things upstairs she'd decided weren't attached to memories.

She made her way back up to the attic and dove into sifting through boxes. For the next couple of hours, the mindless cataloging distracted her. Until she opened a trunk and found inside a treasure map sitting on top of an eye patch and a Jolly Roger flag. Damn it. Where was Jonathan? It was almost three. She let irritation slide in. It helped fill the hole growing in her chest and gave her a new focus. Apparently, he wasn't as serious as he claimed about talking or helping.

FIVE

JONATHAN ALTERNATED HIS ATTENTION BETWEEN HIS laptop, his cell phone—which was currently on speaker, sitting on the desk in his hotel room—and the muted Weather Channel. He only meant to return a couple of calls, but one follow-up led to another and created yet more issues. Now the clock crept up on four. The National Weather Service upgraded the incoming tropical storm to a hurricane, and the roads to the Keys would close again soon. Ride this out in his hotel room and piss Bailey off, or potentially lose a multi-million-dollar connection with the vendor they were talking to? He wanted to call her, but only had Nana's landline number. Bailey might answer, but it would be hard to call while he was still on the phone. *Fuck.*

"With the supply issues, we can't offer delivery

for three more weeks," someone said, catching his attention.

Jonathan turned back to the phone conversation. "The deadline was last Thursday." He let an edge of warning slide into his words.

"I get that, but sometimes things like weather have an unforeseen impact."

That was an understatement. He glanced at the TV and the large swirl of satellite imaging over the southern part of the peninsula. The digital radar image filled him with a dread he couldn't shake. A lingering ill-ease from when he was younger. Why the fuck did there have to be a hurricane now? Out of season? While he was here?

His Skype chimed, pulling his gaze back to his computer.

I thought you hung up. Why are you still online? Liz asked.

He typed out a response. *I have to handle this first.*

I've got it covered, she said. *Go, or I'll kick you off the conference line.*

He smiled. *You're not the moderator.*

"I'm sorry to interrupt." Liz seized a pause in the conversation. "Jonathan needs to drop off the call."

Don't you dare. He clacked the keys harder than he intended, grinding his teeth the whole time.

She kept talking. "He's dealing with his grandmother's estate and needs to tie up some loose ends this week."

A chorus of sympathy chimed through his speaker, and he sighed. *You set me up.* He clenched and unclenched his fingers, but it didn't stave off his tension. Ten more minutes—that was all he needed to wrap this up. But he couldn't stay on the call after a sendoff like that.

Liz replied, *You're welcome. Go. Don't call back until you're officially on the clock again.*

As if there was any way he'd keep his distance for that long. He'd make sure she couldn't cock block him next time. He wished everyone a good afternoon and hung up. He hated the idea of leaving any issue unresolved, but he had to walk away for the evening, after what Liz said.

He could make it back to the Keys before the storm warning went into effect. He swallowed the discomfort that churned inside at the thought of being stranded out there during a hurricane. Nothing to do for it, and he needed to move past the old memories anyway. He grabbed a change of clothes and moments later was on the road again. Getting out of town was easy. Everyone headed in the opposite direction, so he had no traffic to contend with. He made a quick stop for groceries, and was on his way again.

The several miles of highway running over the

water gave his mind a chance to wander. His mother hated this part of the drive in the summers. It was part of the reason his parents said they weren't vacationing out here anymore when Jonathan was fourteen. He refused to dwell on the fact he almost drowned the year before, or acknowledge that had anything to do with their decision. The larger part was that his father and Nana didn't get along.

On top of that, fourteen years old was when Jonathan advised his father to pull out most of his clients' investments, as they related to the dot-com bubble. Dad didn't think a kid knew anything about the market, and months later, lost millions as the crash spread and consumed more and more tech startups. Which was about the time Jonathan took the money he'd saved, bought himself a bus ticket to Florida, and ran away to live with Nana.

He shook the memories aside. The reminder of bad business deals made him itch to dial back into the conference call. He restrained himself with the decision to check in tonight, once Bailey left for the evening. There was a ninety-nine percent chance the storm would pass around them, leaving nothing more than light rain in its wake, and tomorrow they'd be done with this damn road-closure business.

He cranked the stereo, to drown out any more mental rambling, and let the shock of metal guitar rattle his skull. It was almost five when he parked in front of the house. Clattering and banging from above greeted him when he stepped inside. At least Bailey was still here. Something crashed into the floor overhead, shaking the room. "Bailey?" He dropped the groceries and sprinted upstairs, pulse hammering in his ears when she didn't answer.

Another house-rumbling boom greeted him. "*Bailey?*" He climbed the attic ladder as quickly as he could. Why wasn't she answering? Had she hurt herself? Did something fall on top of her? A bare bulb hung from the ceiling, casting long shadows around the room and blending with the evening light.

"*What?*" Her irritated question came from behind him.

He spun and found her standing in the middle of stacks of boxes. Strands of hair had come loose from her ponytail and flew in wisps around her face, and dirt smudged her cheeks. His hammering heart slammed into his ribs. Despite the pursed lips and pink flush of exertion, she looked—

Furious. Nothing more. He cut off all other notions. "I heard a series of crashes. I was worried."

"I'm surprised you made it back to hear anything. I figured you'd hole up until the storm blew over, rather than risk getting stuck here again."

"I got held up. Things happen. I don't have to

be here." He clenched his jaw. This wasn't how he wanted this conversation to go.

She scrubbed her face and moved closer. "I didn't mean to go off on you. I'm glad you made it."

"That was almost an apology. Are you feeling all right?" He held his hand to her forehead, and she swatted it away, a smile peeking through her scowl.

"Bozo."

He grabbed her fingers, and a jolt raced through him, sliding along his skin and lighting up his nerve endings. He pushed the reaction aside and tugged her toward the ladder. "I brought iced tea. Come downstairs, cool off, and we'll talk."

"No." Despite the protest, she didn't pull away. "I let you talk me into that last night, though I'll admit I wanted to be convinced. But I'm a day behind because of it. So now you're going to grab one of these boxes, and then another, and help me sift through everything, while I apologize."

He studied her face—her crystal blue eyes, staring back; dirt-smeared freckles; full lips, half-pouting in the middle of her smile. Not furious. Simply beautiful. Letting his gaze drift lower—over a tank-top that hugged perky breasts, and faded jeans that followed the curve of her legs—would be a mistake. "Don't do that."

Bailey let her fury grow for hours, while she sifted through contents of the room. Heat and dust amplified her irritation, as countless minutes ticked away and Jonathan still didn't show. When the stack of boxes tumbled down on her, slamming her square between the shoulders, she snapped and kicked the lot of them. She cursed him from here to hell for being too... *something* to come back.

Then he had to rush up here, concern etched on his face, and be worried about her well-being. It disrupted her anger and knocked her off balance.

"Don't do what?" she asked.

He took one of the boxes nearby, slid it between them, and crouched next to it. "Don't apologize." The flaps scraped against each other when he pulled them apart.

"But—"

"There's bottled water downstairs. It's still cold. Go grab one, so you don't get a heatstroke or dehydration."

Controlling. Arrogant. Despite his annoying command, his distress over her well-being made her insides flutter. "I'm not—"

"*Go.*" He looked up from the contents of his box.

She huffed but didn't have a reasonable argument. And water did sound good. She brushed past him. When she got downstairs, she found two plastic bags of groceries spilled across the entryway. He really had been worried. She smiled in spite of herself, stashed the food, and grabbed two bottles to take upstairs. When she moved behind Jonathan, mischief and the tiniest hint of spite snaked through her.

He was focused on a collection of trinkets in front of him. "Welcome back."

"Thanks." She dragged the chilled bottle along the back of his neck.

He let out a long groan that blended into a laugh and reached back for the water. "So mean."

"Maybe. But you're bossy."

"Yup. And you love it."

She strolled back to where she'd been working, twisted the top off the drink, and took a long swallow. She finished half of it before she was ready to admit he was right. She needed that. She realized he was watching her, a smile playing on his face. "I do not," she said.

"You have a system in place. How is this all arranged?"

She nodded at the different sections of the room she'd already organized. "Trash goes to the left, stuff to keep to the right, and sellables in the middle. And why shouldn't I apologize?" She refused to be distracted from the original point of the conversation.

"Because you don't mean it." He moved the box to her *sellable* location, then grabbed another one.

Measure her response or bite back? "What I didn't mean were the things I said last night."

"You did." His even, infuriating tone was one she recognized after all these years. He was working hard to keep his thought and emotion in check. "We both know the liquor doesn't make up anything except the notion that what's already there is okay to say."

She wasn't interested in being analyzed. "Your note said you wanted to talk. Was that simply to berate me?"

"No. But I don't want to gloss over it with false platitudes and *I didn't mean it* and *it was the booze speaking.*" His expression cracked, and a mixture of sadness and amusement slid in.

She'd never seen him break before, but it *had* been a long time. "Then what's the point?" She dug into the next crate. Stacks of clothing. She started a new pile across the room. "To donate."

"Admit it happened, don't hide from it, and move on."

That was entirely too reasonable. Rain drove against the siding, rattling its agreement.

"And now that's out of the way..." He trailed off when he looked inside a wooden crate. "Oh." He sank back to the floor, and dust rose around him.

"What is it?"

"Nothing. To sell." He pushed the lid back on

and shoved the box away. It screeched across the wood.

Curiosity piqued, she pried open the top again. Inside was corrugated cardboard and bubble wrap. She reached for a piece on top of the pile, and he grabbed her wrist. It didn't take much effort to shake off his grip. She pulled off the wrapping, to reveal a delicate China saucer. "Pretty."

"Put it away." An edge lined his words.

Confused and concerned, she looked at him. "What's up with you?"

Thunder crashed. Lightning brightened the room for a flash before the window darkened again. Drops of water splattered against the glass. "Donate it if it's not worth anything."

"Tell me." She set the plate on top of the wrapped dishes. She wasn't sure why it was important, but she needed an explanation.

The emotion vanished from his face, and the blank nothing rushed back in. "Not a big deal. Family heirloom. She was saving it for my wedding. Doesn't hold the same meaning if she's not here to —" He shook his head. "What's next?"

Bailey swore she felt the grief spill from him. "I'm sorry."

"See, now I believe you." His smile was weak. He pushed the crate to the other side of the room, somewhere between the *donate* and *keep* piles. The storm kicked up, and gales slammed into the side of the house.

Would every other stack of belongings bring this much pain? It was going to be a long week. She nodded at the boxes that fell on her earlier. "Those attacked me. They're probably next."

They worked in silence for a while, raindrops against the roof taking the place of conversation.

"How long do you want us working, boss?" Jonathan's question startled her.

With the storm, it was hard to tell what time of day it was, but if the sun hadn't set yet, it was close. She made a show of looking around the room. "We got a lot done. I guess we can call it a night." And she desperately wanted to wash the grime from her face and arms.

"I'm making dinner. Are you staying?" He stood and offered her a hand up. His grip was firm and warm. Enticing, in a way she refused to linger on.

She pulled away as soon as she had her footing. It was tempting to tease him about macaroni and cheese not being a real meal, but she saw the ingredients he bought—noodles, cream, mushrooms, and more. While she wasn't sure what he was going to make, it was fancier than pre-packaged. "I'd like that. Let me clean up a little bit first, and I'll be right down."

In the bathroom, the cool water poured over her hands and wrists, chasing the heat away but not erasing the invisible imprints of Jonathan's touches. She splashed her face and scrubbed at the dirt smudges. She was a mess.

"Ale?" His voice carried up the stairs.

The nickname made her growl when anyone in town used it. Coming from him, it drew a smile without her permission. "Yeah?"

"Where's the steak?"

"There was no steak." She dried herself off and made her way downstairs. She found him on his knees near the front door, peering under the couch.

"Fuck." He reached for something, and seconds later pulled out a paper-wrapped bundle. One corner looked chewed on. "I guess I should be grateful that damned cat can't fit under there."

That must be the missing meat. "I didn't see it."

"I figured you didn't leave it down there on purpose." He smiled. He peeled the paper, sniffed, studied the contents for a moment, and then shook his head. "It might still be good, but I'm not willing to risk it in this heat and humidity. I don't think I can make beef Stroganoff without the beef."

Her stomach grumbled, reminding her she skipped lunch in her fit of irritation. She could offer up the cold cuts in the fridge, but what he was making sounded a lot better. "I have hamburger at home. It's not quite the same, but the rain stopped. We could walk over there."

"Leave the ghosts of the past behind for now?"

He'd still be there. And she only owned the property because she got it in the divorce. She was worn out from shoving memories aside. "There are still ghosts. They're just different ones."

"I'll take that. Besides, *dinner at Bailey's house* was always one of my favorite parts of summer."

SIX

Jonathan was struggling. In the last day, he'd met three different versions of Bailey. The girl he hung out with in the summer—best friend, confidant, and link to sanity when his home life was falling apart—was the image he wanted to cling to and kept reinforcing it in his mind. Then there was the eighteen-year-old, who told him in no uncertain terms that she never wanted to see him again and hoped he rotted in whatever Godless hell he ended up in. He was doing the best he knew how, to keep from summoning her, and failing about half the time.

And on rare occasion, the woman Bailey was now shone through. Laughing. Witty. And God-damn fuckable.

She walked a few feet ahead, facing him, rarely looking behind her, to check her step. The warm breeze whipped her hair around her face, no matter how many times she tried to tuck the loose strands away. "The little boy thinks about Dad's answer for a minute, then says, *Dad, I think the UPS guy wants to buy mom.*" As she told her joke, the corners of her mouth tugged up in a barely suppressed smile.

Even if the punchline didn't get him, her laugh would have been infectious. "Okay, I yield." He held up his hands in false surrender. "Auctioneers can be funny too."

"Told you so."

"Do you do most of your business in Miami?" he asked.

She screwed her face into a sour expression. "When I have to, but Atlanta's my standard destination."

That was a twelve- to thirteen-hour drive. "Are the auction houses better up there?"

"Eh... Yes. No. I guess? What about you? What's L.A. like?"

"Back up. What's Atlanta got over Miami?"

"Nothing. Personal preference. Don't worry about it."

"It's almost like you want me to ask." He never would have questioned it, if she wasn't so quick to change the subject. The sharp tang of the ocean lingered in the air, reminding him this was only a break in the rain; it wasn't done yet. With the orange glow of the setting sun behind Bailey, he was treated to a stunning view.

"It's a lot of things." She whirled away from him and slowed her pace until they walked side by side. "The people are different up there. I have more solid contacts. I like the big-city feeling. The clubs are better."

"You go dancing?"

"Dancing. Picking up guys I'll never see again."

That image wasn't going to leave him alone anytime soon. Bailey swaying to the music. Grinding. Flushed. Lost in the beat. "What?"

"You heard me." She glanced sideways, a smirk on her full lips.

Fucking hell. A wave of possessiveness washed through him, but it was tempered by fantasy. Picturing himself as the random guy she teased. Feeling her up on the dance floor. Finding a dark corner and making her squirm. His cock strained against his jeans, and he tried to be subtle about adjusting himself. "I like the sound of it. I wanted to see if you'd repeat it." Not the way to dial the conversation back.

Her playful sideways glance said she didn't mind. "One-night stands. I hit up a club, find an anonymous guy, get laid, and go our separate ways."

"So wicked." He tried to push the images out of his mind with his exhale. It didn't work.

"You disapprove."

"Not that my opinion of your free time matters, but no. I like it."

"Now who's wicked?"

A drop of rain hit his nose, and another his cheek and arm. The warm rain didn't ease the heat flowing over his body. "You don't get an exclusive claim on *naughty*."

"Which is good. Imagine how dull life would be if I were the only one." She peeked up at him through her eyelashes. "What about you?"

"What about me?"

"You're no stranger to the casual hookup." The sky opened up and dumped down sheets of water, soaking them both in seconds. She closed her eyes and turned her face up.

He refused to let the sudden rain and the past it summoned rattle him, despite the way it threatened to steal his good mood. She was a much better focal point. He wasn't sure which captivated him more— her awe or the way her wet top accentuated every inch of her torso, down to the perky nipples. He forced his attention back to her face. Definitely her awe.

"Will you think less of me if I tell you I've never sought it out?" he asked, though for the first time in a long time, he was considering a one-night stand.

"Too busy working?" She quirked her mouth in amusement.

He had the occasional girlfriend, but they never

cared for his schedule, and it'd been years since he had time to go on the prowl. "Guilty as charged. At least one of us is getting laid."

"That's one way to look at it." She laughed.

They reached her front porch, and the awning took the storm from them. She unlocked the house and let them in. "Wait here. I'll go grab some towels."

A small square of tiles sat inside the door, with a mat on it. He did his best to keep the water from dripping on the carpet, and watched her ass until she vanished into another room of the ranch-style house.

She returned seconds later and threw him a fluffy towel. "Catch."

"Thanks." He wiped away the excess water, but only took his gaze from her to dry his face.

She tossed her head forward to dry her hair, and he caught a glimpse of a purple glare peeking above her tank top. He traced his fingers over the bruise. "What happened?"

A soft groan escaped her throat, and she leaned back into his touch. "The crash you heard earlier? Hit me in the back."

"Looks nasty." He trailed his touch down her soft skin, as he pulled more of the shirt back. "You should ice it." With each new contact, her sighs drilled deeper inside, jolting his senses, and tugging at his cock. Damn it, he wanted her.

"I'll be fine. Do you want the shower first?" She spun to face him.

He rested a palm on her cheek, forcing her gaze to his. Reason argued this was a bad idea. *Fuck reason.* It was only for one night. Neither of them had illusions to the contrary. "Or we could share."

She laughed but cut it short and caught her bottom lip between her teeth. He drew his thumb along her mouth, tugging her lip loose. So fucking alluring. Every inch of him begged him to dip his head and capture her mouth.

———

Bailey thought Jonathan was joking, until she took a second look. The want in his eyes. The tension vibrating through his grip, despite his gentle touch. She was used to being the hunter. This was different. And dangerously tantalizing. "To save water? Is this a conservation thing?" It took more effort than she expected, to keep the joke in her words.

"If that's what you want to call it." Each time he dragged his thumb across her skin, sparks sped through her thoughts, erasing reason.

"What would you call it?" she asked.

He stood so close, she was surprised the fire burning between them didn't turn the water on their clothes into steam. "Sating a desire.

Quenching a thirst. Making up for lost time. I'm not too picky about terminology, as long as it involves me stripping you down and exploring your body."

"I don't…" She couldn't finish the protest. Her body tingled in anticipation. If she leaned closer, their lips would meet. She'd feel his hard body against hers. Desire spilled inside. This was the biggest mistake she could possibly make right now. Bits of her still cared about him; the parts she tried to ignore since he showed up yesterday meant this wasn't meaningless for her. But he wasn't looking at it that way. He hadn't shown any interest beyond staring, until she brought up the one-night stands. This was only sex for him.

"Don't what? Don't want to get involved? You said it yourself last night—I'm leaving in a few days. This isn't a long-term agreement. Or maybe you're implying you don't do one-night stands. I was listening, and that's not true. You don't think you're interested? I'll reference last night again." He stepped back, hands up, putting a few inches between them. "Though you may have changed your mind."

His logic confirmed her suspicions. This was a physical encounter, nothing more. But freaking hell, she wanted him close again. Wanted another kiss like last night's, but with the power of sobriety behind it. Wanted to know what he felt like. She was willing to bandage her heart later if it meant having him now. "I don't think the shower is the best place for something like that."

He chuckled as he rested his palm on the base of her neck, to pull her closer. "It's a starting point." He kissed her hard, holding her head captive and claiming her mouth. His tongue danced out to meet hers, probing and hungry. The scent of rain lingered on his skin, mixing with the faint musk of his cologne and teasing her thoughts.

Summoning the brain power to form words, she broke the kiss. She almost dove back in when he frowned, a question heavy in his dark eyes. "Bathroom's this way," she said. When she grabbed his hand, his warm grip sent a rush of desire pulsing through her. "Shower?"

"Right. Getting clean. That's what we're doing." The moment they were in the small room, he pressed his lips to hers again. Nipping became a consuming crush of skin against skin.

She needed to feel more. When she tugged at the bottom of his shirt, wet fabric slid against her palms, teasing and tempting.

He broke away, to let her pull the clothing off and toss it aside. "Impatient?" he asked, diving back to her lips as soon as the path was clear, then kissing along her jaw and down her neck. He moved his hands to her waist, under her top and against her bare skin. The heat of his grip obliterated clammy chill.

She tilted her head with a sigh. Every kiss, nibble, and touch drew her further into the invisible bubble around them. The one cutting them off from reality. "We have to get out of the wet clothes. Otherwise we'll catch something."

"Hmm…" His lips vibrated against the hollow of her throat. "Practical. I like that." In a fluid motion, he yanked her shirt over her head, then pulled her to him again. His bare chest against her body seared through all of her.

She reached back, to unhook her bra, and let it fall into the growing pile of clothes. The humid air on her bare skin soothed already-hard nipples. He cupped her breasts, chasing away the cold. "You need to be warmed up." A smile tugged at the corners of his mouth.

"What did you have in mind?"

He kneaded one breast, and the numbness of cold rapidly evaporated. He lowered his head and took the other nipple in his mouth. Arousal sparked through her, growing when he sucked hard on the swollen nub. She squeezed her thighs together, but it didn't quench the growing throb between her legs.

When he broke away, disappointment welled inside Bailey. "What's wrong?"

"Nothing at all." He kissed her lower lip before spinning away to turn on the shower. "It'll be warmer in there."

"Of course." She wasn't sure she cared, as long

as she could press against him again. They shed the rest of their clothing. She looked down the length of his body, memorizing every line of definition, from his strong chest to the fine trail of blond hair leading down his stomach, to an impressive... asset. She forced her gaze back up, to find him studying her with as much intensity as she'd directed at him. She liked that look.

He shook his head and prompted her to join him in the tub and under the hot stream of water. With a twist, he positioned her to face away from him. He trailed his lips up her back, along the shoulder blades. "I'm still worried about this bruise."

"I'm fine." His concern sank into her senses as deeply as his touch, mingling and amplifying everything. If he'd done this thirteen years ago, instead of leaving... She shook the thought aside. The past was her mistake. She couldn't blame him. Besides, this was temporary, as it should be.

"I still think we should keep the pressure off it." He danced his fingers over the tender skin, and then pulled her close, so her back rested against his chest. "We'll have to be gentle." He reached around her to grab the body wash and squirted a dollop in his hand.

Her anticipation spiked, turning her body into a quivering wire, waiting for the right contact in order to find release. "I don't really do *gentle*."

"Only with your back." He settled his palms against her stomach. The shock of the cold soap quickly vanished. He found her nipples again and pinched hard, drawing a groan and sent a pulse straight to her core. The sharp cherry of the soap mingled with hints of pain, chasing away the exhaustion of the long day. Each time he tugged and tweaked, she ground into him. His cock dug into her ass. She tried to face him, wanting something to grip and needing an outlet for the pleasure filling her.

He held her firm. "Not yet. We're getting clean."

The slippery desire between her thighs disagreed. "Is that what this is?" she asked.

"Mhm." He slipped his hands along her body with the help of the body wash, gliding over her stomach, along her butt cheeks, down her legs, and then back up. He drew close to her aching sex but never met it. By the time he stood again and circled her waist with one arm, she was ready to burst, hovering at the edge of climax, her body pleading to be pushed over. She heard the *click* of plastic on plastic, and seconds later, the cascade of water hit her from a new angle. He'd removed the shower-head, to rinse the soap away.

The slow, teasing seduction was sweet. Pleasant. A type of attention she could get addicted to if she wasn't careful. She wanted rough, fast, and desperate. A frozen moment in time to cling to and then let vanish when it was over. She was barely aware of her hand creeping down her stomach, seeking a way to offer release.

"No touching." A growl cut through his words. He grabbed her wandering wrist tight enough that she sucked a sharp breath of surprise through her teeth.

That was about billion times more intoxicating than the gentle. The sting of his fingers digging into her skin amplified the heavy tension humming inside. "Please?" She didn't mean for the whimper to slip out, but it was too late to take it back. She heard the *clack* of the shower nozzle returning to its home.

His chuckle was haunting and tantalizing. "Please, what?"

"Finger me. Fuck me. Stop teasing, and let me come."

"I like the way that sounds." He captured her free arm too, and held both behind her back with one hand.

Before she could decide if she wanted to twist free, he dipped his fingers between her legs. The sensual seduction was gone. He focused on her clit, stroking the swollen bud. A spasm spilled through her at the contact, and her legs wobbled. This wasn't the gentle touch he covered her with moments earlier. He pushed hard and stroked the sensitive button, changing his pace as her cries grew more frantic and punctuated. Climax swelled inside and tumbled her into light-headed euphoria. She thrust against his hand, until his touch became too much. When she shuddered from his touch, he eased up but didn't pull away. Instead, he grabbed the shower head again and glided his fingers along her slit, rinsing and applying enough pressure to keep her thoughts muddled and her body humming, without it being too much.

It was fortunate this was a one-time thing. She'd get hooked fast on playtime like this. As long as she pushed him away at the end of the night though, it wouldn't be a problem.

SEVEN

JONATHAN DIDN'T KNOW THE LAST TIME HE'D BEEN so hard. His dick ached from holding back. Bailey insisted he had to be clean too, and every time she slid her hand along his shaft, he had to stop her so he didn't come. They finished the shower and toweled off.

She draped her arms around his neck, molded her body to his, and shifted her weight to torment him. "If the shower is just a starting point, what now?" she asked.

He knotted his fingers in her hair, holding her head captive so he could look her in the eye. "I need to bury myself inside you. Feel you wrapped around my cock. Watch you ride me, and see your face when you come."

"Bedroom's over there." She gestured behind her.

He barely had the presence of mind to grab a condom from his wallet.

She raised her brows, a smile dancing on her face. "Why are you carrying protection if you don't make a habit of this?"

"A boy scout is always prepared." Hands on her hips, he guided her toward the other room.

"You weren't a boy scout. What was it you said? *If I'm going to work hard for recognition, I want a paycheck, not an embroidered little badge.*"

He laughed at her false baritone. "Fine. It's because I'm male, so even when I'm not actively looking to get laid, there's always a part of me that hopes."

"Fair enough." She paused next to the bed and faced him. Her bottom lip was caught between her teeth, and pink still flushed her skin from the hot water. Fuck, she was gorgeous.

He kissed her, searing the sensation of her soft lips into his thoughts. Each moan and gasp she made acted like a string connected to his cock. She plucked the condom from between his fingers, and without breaking away, rolled it into place. The smooth motion made him grit his teeth in anticipation.

She glided his cock head along her slit. She was already slippery again. God, he couldn't do this. He spun them both, so he could sit on the edge of the bed, and pulled her to straddle his legs. Instead of lowering herself, she hovered, the heat of her center teasing him. He wasn't going to last at all once he sank into her, and he wanted to draw this out a little longer. He dropped his thumb to her clit and rubbed lightly. She squirmed and tried to pull away, but he gripped her thigh, holding her in place. She twisted and moaned. Dug her nails into his arms, rather than try to escape. Her eyelids fluttered, and a cry tore from her throat when she came again.

He thrust up when her grip tightened, and groaned at the sudden penetration. He slammed inside her, as her pussy clenched around him. In the back of his mind, he wondered if she might break the skin with her nails. He didn't care. His head swam each time he plunged deep, and lights danced across his vision. Orgasm cascaded through him, but he didn't slow down. He couldn't slow his pounding inside her until he was spent and the edge of intensity tapered off.

He matched his rhythm to hers, slowing and then stopping as she did. She leaned forward until she rested her head on his chest, still straddling him. As he softened, he slipped out of her. The only sound in the room was the downpour of rain mixed with their efforts to catch their breath. Her cheek was hot against his skin, teasing and comforting.

He trailed his fingers through her hair, watching the pale strands flutter down against the dim light. "I think I owe you dinner."

"Aren't you supposed to do that before, not after?" Her laugh fluttered through him.

"Am I? I guess I need a little more practice, to get this right. Either way, I think the rain ruined the noodles on the way over here."

She rolled off him and curled up next to his side, head on his arm. "I don't think your Stroganoff was meant to be."

"I still owe you dinner." He kissed the top of her head before extracting himself. A nagging inside wanted him to stay wrapped up with Bailey, and that was the exact reason he wouldn't. "Permission to raid your kitchen for something else?"

For a moment her smile looked sad, but it cheered before he could think about it too much. She sat, making no attempt to cover up. "If you insist."

Unable to stop himself, he leaned in one more time and stole another quick, hungry kiss. "Meet me downstairs when you're ready." He strode from the room before she could reply. Hanging around would either lead to playful teasing, or another round of fighting, and both seemed like a bad idea.

He paused in the bathroom doorway, *of course* repeating in his head when he saw his clothes in a wet pile by the tub. His bag was back in his car. Apparently, he was destined to spend large parts of this trip wandering around in almost nothing.

BAILEY FLOPPED onto her back and stared at the ceiling. Being alone in the room tugged at her from so many directions. It gave her a chance to make sure her legs worked, which she wasn't complaining about. That wobbly feeling helped keep her in a pleasant fuzzy afterglow… it might have been a lot more pleasant if he were still with her. A good reminder it was time to close the door on whatever happy emotions she had and lock them away where they belonged.

She walled off her heart, ignoring the throb behind her ribs, and sat up. How long would it take Jonathan to remember he didn't have dry clothes to wear? She grabbed some things from her dresser and wandered into the bathroom, to clean up. He'd draped their wet items over the shower rod. The sight made her smile. Fortunately, the washroom was at the back of the house, so tossing his things in the dryer gave her another few minutes to collect her thoughts.

After taking care of that, she dressed and grabbed an extra pair of shorts and a T-shirt from her bottom drawer. Voices floated into the room, and she frowned. Was he talking to someone? That wasn't Jonathan. It sounded muffled. No, he was watching TV. Something about that bothered her. She padded toward the noise, and stalled in the doorway when she realized what had his attention. The Weather Chanel.

"Sorry." He didn't look up from the screen. "I couldn't get a signal on my phone, and I had to see…" He shook his head and stood. The only thing covering him was a towel around his waist. "I'll get started on dinner." Tension that wasn't there before ran through his voice, and his gaze drifted back to the screen every time he started to look away.

They were showing radar images of the area. The hurricane had been upgraded again in the last few hours, to a Category 4. The tip of it had caused flash flooding throughout the Keys, including overtaking some of the smaller bridges, and wind tore older structures down as it gusted north. "Looks like I'll be here for at least a couple more days, regardless my plans." His words were strained, and she suspected it wasn't all caused by the possible loss of access to work.

Was he paler, or was that a side effect of the lighting? Over the last thirty years or so, she'd ridden out a lot of hurricanes. Like most locals, she was unfazed by them. There was one that still haunted her dreams, though. When they were thirteen, it happened a lot like this. The weather said *no big deal*, and she'd never seen a big storm. She convinced Jonathan they didn't need to go home yet, and despite his parents calling for him, she and

Jonathan stayed out on the beach and in the ocean, playing.

"Hey. I grabbed you some clothes." She nudged his arm, to distract him from the news.

He took the shorts and T-shirt but didn't look away from the TV. "Thanks."

She could almost guarantee what was going through his mind. The same thing she saw in her head. Back then, the storm drove in quickly, the wind picking up and turning splashes to roaring waves that slammed into the sand. He got swept up in them, and by the time rescuers pulled him out, he wasn't breathing. Despite how long ago it happened, the memory still terrified her. Was it doing the same to Jonathan? It took almost a minute to bring him back with CPR. Bailey's parents didn't try and pull her from his side. He and she spent the night in the local clinic, listening to Jonathan's parents scream at Nana about teaching the kids to be irresponsible, and threatening to never let Jonathan see her again.

When his family left a few days later, Bailey was terrified she'd never see him again.

She dragged herself back to the now. "Hurricane party?" Her chipper tone sounded tinny and false when it hit her eardrums. "I've got tequila and sweet-and-sour mix."

"No drinking." He gave her half his attention. As soon as the anchor said something about eighty-mile-an-hour gusts driving into the coast, he snapped his head back to the news.

She tugged at his arm, to prompt him to turn toward her. "Get dressed, at least."

"Right." He shook his head and focused on the clothes. "Am I wearing another guy's leftovers?"

"They're mine." She took the opportunity to grab the remote and turn off the TV.

"I want that on in the background."

"You don't, and it won't change anything. Get dressed."

"Now who's bossy?" He held up the shorts, and looked between her and the clothing. "These are too big for you."

"They weren't, once upon a time." Would her brushoff deter him? She didn't want to explain why she had them. Not now, not ever—to him or anyone.

He glanced back at the blank screen. "Okay."

She'd spill whatever it took, to keep him distracted. "Put them on. Don't touch the remote. And sit. When I come back, I'll tell you why I have them." As soon as she made the commitment, she wanted to take it back. There were a billion other ways to pass the time that didn't involve gutting herself in front of someone else. But this was the best reminder of why no man was worth losing her heart over, no matter how good a past they shared.

EIGHT

IT WASN'T THAT JONATHAN WAS WORRIED ABOUT THE weather. He wanted to watch for purely academic reasons—to know if he'd have cell-phone access again soon; to get an idea of when he could head back to the mainland. His fascination with the glaring swirl of the radar maps had nothing to do with the heavy weight trying to force the air from his lungs. Didn't correlate at all to the dreams he never managed to shake, from which he woke up struggling to breathe past the water and choking on his inability to fight the currents.

He forced himself to swallow, and then tugged on the clothes Bailey brought him. He was grateful her promise to explain gave him a new direction for his thoughts.

She returned a moment later with a bag of potato chips, a jar of onion dip, and two cans of

Coke. "Dinner is served." She arranged everything on the coffee table.

"Not quite what I was going for." He settled back onto the couch.

She took the spot next to him and twisted sideways so she faced him, one knee propped on the couch and resting against his leg. "Unless you can turn hamburger, two pickles, and sweet-and-sour mix into something gourmet, you wouldn't have done much better. I don't keep a lot in my kitchen."

"Why not?"

"A list of reasons. I travel as much as I'm home. I don't like to cook. It's too much temptation—" She snapped her jaw shut. "*Angel investor firm*—how's that work?"

"People pitch me ideas that aren't necessarily worth millions, but are still solid business plans, and I loan them money in return for a share of the profits. Why do you own clothes three sizes too big for you?"

She grabbed one of the soda cans and fiddled with it, not popping the top. "If I tell you, you have to promise not to check the weather again until tomorrow morning. And that doesn't mean midnight; it means normal wake-up time."

She was trying to distract him. The realization threatened to make him smile. Not that he needed distracting. "I promise."

"When I married Danny, things were wonderful.

I *knew* you were wrong about him." Bailey's words cut deep.

"I see." Despite him knowing *something* went wrong, Nana never told him what. Said it wasn't her place. At eighteen years old, for the second time in his life, he thought he'd never see Bailey again. Not because of some great tragedy—though he swore it was one, at the time—but because she was engaged and refused to listen when Jonathan tried to tell her Danny was a cheating, lying asshole.

Each time she clicked the tab on her drink with her nail, metal clinked against metal. "And then, about six months in, life imploded. I was dropping something off for a friend who worked at one of the hotels, and found him sucking face with a brunette in the bar." When she opened the drink, a hiss mixed with her words. She took a long swallow. "I should have gotten furious—that was what I felt. But I told him I'd see him at home, so quietly I'm not sure he heard me. I called in to work, went home, and stared blankly at the wall, trying to figure out what to do, until he showed up about three hours later."

"He didn't even have the balls to follow home right away? Chase you down as you left?" Fury surged inside Jonathan. A rage he thought he'd put behind him years ago.

Bailey gave a bitter laugh. "Save the pissed-off-edness—and don't tell me that's not a word. We're just getting started." She grabbed the chips and nibbled one. "He was all sweetness and apology, and even brought me chocolates. Told me he was so sorry. He loved me. It was a lapse in reason. The moment he saw me, he knew he didn't want to lose me. Swore he hadn't been with anyone else since we got engaged, and it would never happen again. I told him I didn't know if I could trust him now. He said he wanted to earn it back—my trust. We'd work through this. He'd be better. I'd try harder..."

"Try harder at what?" Jonathan wasn't sure he wanted the answer.

She met his gaze, eyes hard and expression blank. "In his words, I *had* put on a couple extra pounds since we got married. We both had things to work toward, and we'd do it together. Wait." She held up a finger when he opened his mouth to argue. "We went back to happy la-la land. It was all good for a few more months—I was starting to trust him again—and then one of his girlfriends called the house. Rinse and repeat this conversation five... six more times? I lost count. The first couple of encounters, Danny was sweet about his apologies. It started with hints. I should take better care of myself. I needed to try harder to make him happy. I didn't understand what he wanted in the bedroom. I was so fucking fat."

Jonathan couldn't remember the last time he was so furious. "Ale, I—"

"Don't." She clipped the word off. "Don't tell me you're sorry. Because you're a decent human being, I assume that, and I don't want your pity. Don't say anything because you feel obliged. You tried to warn me, and what could you have done? You weren't here. It wasn't your responsibility."

"If you told me... If Nana said something..."

"What? You would have hopped the next plane to Florida and beaten the crap out of him? Even if that was true, it wouldn't matter. I would've been furious with you, he'd tell me it was my fault, and the cycle would start over again. While it was happening, I didn't see it for what it was. The entire thing was my fault as I lived it. He tore me down, to the point I was convinced I couldn't do anything right. I gained fifty pounds and hated myself every step of the way. *No wonder he didn't love me. Of course he was sleeping with other women. I was lucky he let me claim to be his wife, anymore.* And you know how they love gossip around here. Everywhere I went, I was the pudgy girl whose husband was sleeping with everyone but her." Venom filled her words, and her voice shook by the time she finished.

Sympathy died in his throat. She didn't want that. Or pity. "How did you get out?"

"Nana." Bailey set the chips aside, though she'd only eaten one. "She kidnapped me."

Under any other circumstance, he'd laugh. Now

the best he could manage was a snort of disbelief. "How'd that work?"

"Danny and I argued one day, and I fought back. It wasn't the first time I'd bitten back, but it was the first time I told him we were done. I walked out, but I didn't have anywhere to go. In the time leading up to that, I'd drifted away from my few local friends. My parents had moved to Tampa. I was scared of what he'd say if I touched the money in our account to get a hotel room. So I went to the coffee shop. Nana found me sobbing in my car. I was terrified he wouldn't take me back, and just as scared this was the only place I had to go and I'd be stuck with him forever."

Bailey dragged the back of her hand across her cheeks, as if to wipe away tears, but Jonathan didn't see any. She dragged in a shaky breath. "She brought me back to her house. Then… she listened. I told her everything I just told you, more or less. She didn't say anything, except to let me know she was listening. She had that damned expression you get."

"I have an expression?"

Bailey almost smiled. "That stupid impassive mask that would make you a brilliant card player. She had the same look. She didn't judge me, or offer her opinion or her advice. She let me ramble as I talked it all through. And then she refused to let me go home. She called Danny. Told him I was staying with her for the week. I begged her not to. What if he didn't let me come home after? He didn't care. Not until I realized at the end of the week I didn't want to go home. While I was there, Nana and I talked about everything. What it was like for her to grow up. You. Me. Danny only came up when I mentioned him.

"I'm not saying a switch was flipped; I still had days *I knew* I was wrong and wanted to go back to him. Times I was terrified I'd be alone forever if I walked away from him. But Nana was there for me through the divorce. Through figuring out how to live alone. Through finding work. That's how I got into the auctioning and appraisal. It felt good, selling off all his shit." She made a sound that was half-sob, half-laugh. "You must think I cry and scream all the time. I promise, in everyday life, I'm pretty even keel."

"I had no idea." He reached out to comfort her. He needed to do something.

She placed her palm on his chest, holding him at arm's length. "Don't. I'll be fine." Tears flowed down her cheeks, but she didn't sob or sniffle. "I need a few minutes. I'll be right back."

Jonathan ached to make things right but didn't have any solutions. He let her walk away, suppressing every urge he had to stop her.

Bailey stood in front of the bathroom mirror, red-rimmed eyes staring back, as cold water spilled over her hands and into the sink. She needed to bring her thoughts back under control. Relaying the story shouldn't have hit her so hard. She'd dealt with it and moved on. She only told it to distract him and remind herself she wasn't that person anymore. It was done and over, and she needed to drag herself from that past.

One thing tried to work its way out during her tale, and she'd struggled to hold it back—the nagging voice that insisted it was all Jonathan's fault. He hadn't tried hard enough to stop her from getting married. He walked away and abandoned her to that life.

What else was he supposed to do? She screamed at him, back them. Forced him away, her command that he go and never speak to her again not leaving room for argument. She splashed more water on her face, trying to shock herself into a more neutral place and chase away the confusion raging inside.

A heavenly smell drifted into the room. Garlic. Onions. Beef? She couldn't identify all of the scents, but their combination made her stomach growl. She stepped into the hallway, and a glance at the clock in her bedroom told her she'd been hiding out for almost half an hour. It didn't feel like nearly that long, but at the same time she might as well have suffered an eternity.

She followed her nose to the amazing concoction calling her, and paused in the kitchen doorway. Jonathan had set the table for two. In the middle of it all sat a bag of chips and a pot of something with the lid still on.

He looked up with a tentative smile. "Dinner's on."

"It's after ten. Isn't it a little late for food?"

"Nope." He held out a chair and gestured to it. "We have to eat sometime, and you skipped lunch."

She didn't have the strength to argue the sweet gesture. "What are we having?" she asked.

He scooted the chair in when she sat. "You were right about your pantry; our options are a little limited. We're having nachos. Sort of." He tilted the chip bag and dumped a generous stack onto her plate, then ladled something over them from the pot. Stroganoff sauce.

He took the spot across from her, and nodded at her plate. "Well?"

She took a tentative bite, and her mouth watered when the first flavors hit her tongue. She paused to say, "It's really good," before shoveling up another scoop.

He glanced at her every few seconds, as they ate. She should be working on distracting him from the storm, but she was caught in the loop of her mistake that was her marriage. The guilt and self-loathing and blame that gnawed at her brain matter.

It was worse that Jonathan no longer wore that freaking poker face she hated so much. Every time he looked up, pity filled his eyes. Or that was concern, but the mess inside refused to believe she deserved that. Several times he opened his mouth, like he wanted to speak, then turned his attention back to his food.

They finished, and he insisted on helping her clean up. When the dishes were rinsed and the leftovers stowed, she stood next to him at the edge of the living room. She couldn't bring herself to make eye contact.

"You can't go out in this weather. I'll show you where the guest room is." She turned in that direction before he could say something. She stopped next to the door, as out of his way as possible, and gestured inside. "The bedding is clean. I'm going to get some sleep. Have a good night."

"Bailey…"

She didn't turn. Pretended she didn't hear his soft request over the wind howling outside. When she reached her room, she flopped on the bed and tried to make out the ceiling in the dark. She wouldn't be sleeping tonight. Not with the onslaught of thoughts tormenting her.

NINE

Between the storm tearing at the world, and Bailey's story echoing in his head, Jonathan spent most of the night tossing and turning. He strained his ears, listening for any sound above the rain hammering against the house. Nothing. Did he have cell coverage yet? If so, he could check into work or at least his mail, since it was still ungodly-o-clock on the west coast. He easily sought out the laundry room at the back of the house, extracted his clothes from the dryer, and then dressed.

He found his phone on the kitchen table. Damn it—still no signal. He wandered into the living room and flipped on the TV. Ambivalence filled him, as he watched the scrolling news and radar map. The hurricane probably wouldn't hit them directly, but they'd catch the edge of it, and that could do significant damage on its own. The highways back to the peninsula were closed. Looked like the Key would be home for the next few days. Once upon a time, that would have been the best news ever. Now, he wasn't sure how he felt about it.

"At least you waited until morning." A tired thread ran through Bailey's cheer.

He spun to face her. Her smile looked as if it took effort, and dark circles sat under her eyes. He wasn't the only one who didn't sleep. "I *did* promise. Storm's supposed to reach full strength by tonight. Do you need help shuttering up?" Should he mention last night? Any of it? Which Bailey would emerge if he did?

"Help would be nice. I'm hoping it doesn't hit hard enough to flood. If you thought cold bathroom tile in the winter was harsh, try stepping out of bed and into several inches of water."

He didn't get a lot of icy tile back home. "You're not staying here," he said.

"Excuse me?" She didn't look upset.

"Nana's house—sorry, *my* house—has metal shutters, and at least one story that probably won't flood. It's safer there."

She twisted her mouth, and then shook her head. "All right, Mr. Bossy. On one condition."

"It's not a negotiation."

"Whatever. If we're going to be stuck there anyway, you're helping me sort through boxes."

And decide which memories were worth keeping and which could be discarded or sold to the highest bidder. "All right."

He found oatmeal in the pantry she'd forgotten about, and made that, while she brewed coffee. Breakfast consumed, they got to tightening up her place as best they could. Sheets of rain slammed into them as soon as they stepped outside.

They made their way from window to window, fighting the wind to close the wooden covers over glass. He held them in place, and she latched down the bars that would keep them there. Furious at their efforts, the weather tore at their clothes and hair, whipping both against their skin.

Jonathan muttered a *thank you* as they reached the second to last stop. He yanked the shutter, and the wind pushed back, jerking it from his hand and slicing the wood across his palm. "*Fuck.*" He pulled back, wiggling his fingers and willing the sting to go away.

"Let me see." Bailey grasped his wrist.

"I'm fine. We need to get this done."

"We have time. Don't pull this macho bull with me... Ouch."

He looked at the wound and was shocked at what he saw. The sharp sting wasn't just a scratch. A deep gash gouged his palm, under the thumb, crimson welling up and being diluting by the rain.

"Come on." She tugged him toward the front door.

"Two windows left. Let's finish."

She pursed her lips. "You need to bandage that."

"And then we'll come out here, the weather will soak through the gauze, and it'll have to be re-wrapped once we're done. The longer you argue, the more it bleeds." Which he didn't want. The pain was becoming a throb.

"Fine. But don't bleed on my shutters." The concern in her voice drowned out the sarcasm.

It was harder than Jonathan expected to do most of the heavy work with his left hand, but keeping the pressure off his right made it easier to hide the wince each time a stab of pain traveled down his arm. Maybe insisting they finish before he took care of the wound *was* macho bullshit.

He waited in the entryway when they finished, so he wouldn't drip on her carpet, while Bailey grabbed gauze, tape, and disinfectant. She joined him again. A numb heat seared him at her tender touch when she examined the cut. She wiped away the excess mess and hissed. "This is deeper than I thought."

"I'm fine." He didn't mind her worry, though. It was reassuring.

"All right. But if your hand turns green and falls off, I'm saying *I told you so.*"

He laughed. "As is your right." He ground his teeth while she slathered the cut with antibiotic salve, relaxing again when she wound the gauze around his hand.

And then she kept wrapping.

"I think you've got it covered," he said.

"I guess. Let me grab a couple things, and we'll head back to your place."

His place. The notion felt foreign, but reality was sinking in. Nana didn't live there anymore. Thunder rolled and boomed overhead, punctuating his thoughts. One more thing to decide. Sell the property? It wasn't as if he was going to live there. He couldn't wrap his brain around letting it go. When he was growing up, Nana's was more like home than home was.

"All set." Bailey joined him again, pulling him back to the now—a far more pleasant place to be, despite the weather.

Fortunately, the shutters on Nana's house pulled down easily and latched in place with minimal effort, so they avoided further injury. They found Lucifer cowering from the storm in the upstairs bathroom, made sure she had food, water, and attention, then let her hide again so they could get back to their sorting.

Once they settled in and started working, things went quickly. Several hours later, they'd gone through almost everything in the attic. The pain in Jonathan's hand dulled, making it easier to ignore whenever he hit it at the wrong angle.

"Have you looked through these yet?" He nodded at a handful of boxes shoved in the corner. The dust on the floor around them was disturbed, but they weren't sitting in any of the piles Bailey'd laid out.

She glanced up, then quickly turned back to the trinkets she was looking through. "No."

The sharp word caught him off guard. "Do I dare?"

"Up to you." And like that, the standoffish switch had been flipped on. She rubbed her face then met his gaze. "I glanced. Open at your own risk—that's all I'm saying."

"Okay..." He flopped next to the shoved-aside grouping and opened the first one. The strong scent of aging, damp paper filled his nostrils, and he wrinkled his nose. When he looked inside, a strange pit welled in his chest. Treasure maps sat on top of a black piece of fabric with white paint. If he unfolded it, he'd see a skull and crossbones. "Oh."

"Yeah. I'm not sure it has any value beyond the sentimental kind." She leaned back, palms on the floor and attention on the box.

The instinct to toss it all spilled through him. It

was from a past that didn't matter now. Instead, he found himself pulling out the top piece of paper and unfolding it with care so it didn't tear. "Did we ever find any of these *treasures*?"

"No. Wait… Maybe one. Remember? That wooden box under the porch, with all the chocolate coins in it?"

He smiled. "I wondered when I got older why she put so much effort into the stories." Something metal clattered to the ground. He set the map aside and grabbed the key. It was corroded and rusted. Welded steel, looking like something that might belong to an ancient lock. Or on a chain around someone's neck. He had no idea if old keys actually looked like this. He held it up. "Perfect example. Why go to all the effort of hiding this up here?"

Bailey furrowed her brow and studied him. "You really think that?"

"Think what?"

"That she made it *all* up."

He returned her puzzled look. "Pirates didn't hide chocolate coins under Nana's back porch. You realize that? And the Easter Bunny isn't real, and neither is Santa?"

"Dork." She tossed a wadded up piece of packing paper at him, and it fell to the ground long before it reached him. "Okay. So she did some of it for you, because you loved the stories. If you resent that or have a problem with it, I'm going to think you don't have a heart."

"I never said that. I'm just wondering. By the time I was ten, I knew the stories weren't real, but she kept telling them." He expected the gnawing inside to turn to pain, but it felt light. Relieved. He realized he was smiling.

Bailey looked amused too. "Who says they're not real? So she enhanced one or two tales. It doesn't mean there's no truth to them."

He gestured to the map he'd unfolded. "Say I follow this, which looks a lot like something straight out of an Indiana Jones movie, and use the magic key. Does that mean I'll find the pirates' buried treasure? As nifty as that idea is, if you're spending your time pillaging the high seas for a living, what kind of long-term investment plan is burying the gold in a box on an island?"

"The reality isn't actually about buried treasure." She laughed. "That part was embellishment; I'm sure. But there's a lot of history here around this being a layover for pirate ships. Back in the late sixteen hundreds—and even later, before colonists figured out how to make their way down here—it was a good stopping point."

"So I can't bank my retirement on this opening a secret treasure chest, worth billions in doubloons?" He gave an exaggerated sigh.

"No. I suppose you'll have to do it through

smart investments and a wicked-scary grasp of the financial market instead. Poor you."

"Sobbing all the way to the bank." He tucked the key into his pocket and dove back into sifting through the contents of the box. He unfurled the *pirate* flag. The paint was chipped and faded, and there was no doubt an inexperienced artist—him— drew and painted the skull. Bailey did the cross-bones underneath. "I'm keeping this, though," he said.

"What are you going to do with it?"

"Hang it behind my desk during tough negotia-tions. What else would I do with it?"

"I don't have a better answer."

Every time she laughed, it filtered through him, chasing away the cobwebs and lingering darkness around why he was here in the first place. He'd do a lot to keep her smiling. The abrupt thought caught him by surprise, and he shoved it aside. Random side effect of the afternoon; that was all that was. As he dug through the box, he found hand drawn maps, homemade eye patches, and a cardboard sword. Most of it was too yellowed and fragile to be worth saving. It ached, for reasons he couldn't explain, to toss it into the trash pile, but he didn't have room for mildewed clutter back home.

Nestled underneath it all, was a small wooden chest. "No way."

"What?"

He pulled it out. It had an ornate carving on the top and sides. An intricate pattern that almost looked Celtic. And it closed with a tarnished brass latch—fragile and held in place with tiny screws. "This." He flipped the clasp and opened the lid. Foil wrappers sat inside. Gold and silver, half-torn and crumpled, and still holding the shape from when they'd been wrapped around candy.

"I can't believe she kept that." Bailey crawled forward, settled next to him, and sifted through the glittery trash. "I can't believe *you* put those back in there."

"Wasn't me." Neither of them bought that. They'd made themselves sick that day, eating an entire box of chocolate. When it came time to clean up, he thought the foil was too pretty to throw out. *God.* He was a sentimental little kid. It was probably a good thing he outgrew that. He emptied the contents into a trash bag.

"What are you doing?"

"It's junk, Ale."

"But…" She sighed. "I know. The box is an antique, though. Hold onto that."

"I don't know what I'd do with it." He set it in the *sell* stack.

She reached across him, pressing her body into his, and grabbed the map. Reluctance filled him when she pulled away again. She folded the paper as carefully as it had been opened, and handed it to him. "The key's useless without this."

"They're stories." Despite his argument, he slipped the paper into the small stack of things he was keeping. "But it'll look good, mounted next to the flag." It wouldn't hurt to hold onto a couple of memories.

TEN

BAILEY SETTLED ONTO THE COUCH, WHILE Jonathan flipped through a shelf of DVDs and VHS tapes. "Does the VCR even still work?" he asked.

"Yup. Guy in town keeps—kept—it running for her. I don't guarantee the tapes are still any good though."

He held up a copy of *Bill and Ted's Bogus Journey*. "That's assuming they ever were."

"She bought that for you." Bailey had enjoyed pretty much the entire day—talking, delving into the past, touching on the present. It made her wonder why she couldn't meet a guy like Jonathan.

He shelved the tape and continued through the stack. "I'm not claiming my taste was perfect, as a kid, but it was better than most people's." Teasing filled his words.

"Is that *Speed 2* I see up there, next to *Spice Girls?*"

They finished going through the attic a few hours ago and agreed they'd tackle his old room tomorrow. After seeing how much he chose to discard, she hated the thought he might throw out most of the toys and models lining the shelves, but it was his stuff. His choice.

He brushed his fingers over the spines of the tapes. "Okay—so I had my questionable moments. I'd still watch either one of them again... but not without a lot more whiskey on hand." He reached the DVDs, and grabbed one of the first in the row. "Now *this* is a classic."

Heat flooded her cheeks when she saw the cover to *American Pie*, not because it was racy, but because it was one of the movies they snuck into, the summer he ran away, and at the meek age of fourteen, she'd never seen anything so raunchy. Unlike the VHS tapes, DVDs were only out for a few years before Jonathan's last trip here.

"I can't believe Nana owned something like that." She managed to keep her voice even.

"This one's all mine. I left it here because my parents were furious when they found out I'd seen it, and watching it again was the perfect rebellion."

Thunder roared, accompanied by a sharp bolt of light, and the house went dark. "I think a higher power's punishing you for your bold disobedience."

"Let Him. Or Her." Jonathan's voice was closer than she expected, and his heat brushed her back. He draped his arms over her shoulders. "Won't stop me from watching it."

She pulled away with reluctance. "Technically, that's exactly what it will do. Not that I'm complaining. Candles and flashlights are in the pantry."

"You don't want to see it?" Jonathan slipped his hand into hers. His bandage was rough against her palm, and the contact was pleasant. They felt their way toward the kitchen.

Her fingertips grazed the cool wood of the pantry door, and she slid it open. "It's not a mixed-company movie." She grasped the flashlight, and mouthed a *thank you* when it flipped on without hesitation. She trained the light on the candles, while Jonathan fetched a handful, and then they returned to the living room.

"You didn't complain the first time we saw it." He placed four candles around the room, lighting them as he went.

She flicked off the flashlight, and the flames cast long, dancing shadows along the walls. Despite the noise slamming into the house, the room got a cozy, almost surreal feeling. She sat on the couch again. "I didn't know what I was walking into. I was humiliated that day, for your information."

"And laughing your butt off. I remember." He

took the spot next to her, close enough his leg rested against hers. "Besides, I'm pretty sure—nope, I'm positive—you were the one telling me last night about how you spend your free time in Atlanta."

Of course he'd bring that up. "That's different."

"How?"

Because you're not there. "It just is."

He nestled a finger under her chin and forced her head up. In the dim light, his eyes were so dark they looked black. She could sink into that gaze.

He licked his lips. "You didn't have a problem with the company last night." His words, smooth and confident, slid under her skin. "Riding my cock. Digging your nails into my arms. How could watching a stranger fuck a pie be more intimate?" His expression shifted to mischievous in an instant.

Her mind scrambled to keep up, but her insides weren't having it. The shared moment in the shower filled her thoughts and sang in her nerves, teasing her with whispers of his skilled fingers roaming her body. She cleared her throat. "We can't watch anything now, so it doesn't matter."

"There's more to it. Isn't there? You've got stories from band camp you kept to yourself."

"I never went to band camp. My fourth grade teacher wouldn't let me play the recorder, because I was out of tune. Those things can't even be tuned, you know."

He dragged his thumb along her jaw so lightly she wasn't sure she felt it. "But you do have stories you've never told me."

Some of them from the wicked thoughts she had after she watched *American Pie*. "Nope. I draw the line at sharing any level of detail about how I did or didn't explore my body as a teenager."

"I don't want details." He drew a finger up her arm, then along her neck, coaxing. "Simply names. Who were you thinking about when you did it?"

She raised her brows. "Celebrities. You." The moment she said it, she wanted to take it back. Or did she?

"This is much better than a movie."

She couldn't argue. "I'm not going to be the only one spilling my secrets. You have to share too."

"I didn't agree to that." He drew a light touch over patches of bare skin—the edge of her ear, the tips of her fingers, the back of her neck. Each new caress teased a little more.

"It's only fair. And don't tell me *life's not fair*."

"That night we kissed on the Fourth. The last time I saw you? I replayed that moment over and over again after I left." His voice dropped an octave, and some of the playfulness faded from his face. "Not only the fight we had, though whenever I had a bad day, that was another mistake from my past that haunted me. I mean the kiss. No woman in college could ever compete with that memory."

The confession stole her breath and fuzzed her thoughts. It wasn't the words, but the way he said them. "Really?" That was intelligent.

"Cross my heart. Last night though, you were better."

Embarrassment filled her, but she pushed it aside. This wasn't a conversation she was backing down from. Like yesterday, boldness pushed her to be direct with Jonathan—a hint of regret she couldn't quite grasp and would rather ignore in favor of this moment. "I've had a little more practice."

"Me too"—he stood, pulled her to her feet, and grabbed a nearby candle—"and I think we should introduce my old bed to how much more experienced we are. Give the springs a work out that's more than a solo act."

"I don't know. I wouldn't mind watching your solo act." She followed him up the stairs.

They reached the room, and he turned to face her. "That only works if we're still sharing." He tugged her inside and stopped short of the bed, then set the candle on the dresser. Long shadows danced along the wall. "Since we're doing this whole *I'll show you mine if you'll show me yours*."

"That's not quite what was going on." Heat flooded her skin, scorching her from head to toe. The thinly veiled suggestion tantalized and terrified her.

"It's an evolving process. We'll run out of spoken secrets sooner or later. If we make the next logical step before that happens, problem solved."

Speaking of steps...her mind was already skipping ahead several, taunting her with images. She didn't know which excited her more—the idea of showing off for him or him being turned on by it. An old insecurity lay on top of it all, adding a layer of bitterness to the fantasy. Any response stalled in her throat.

He trailed his gaze over her face. "Unless you're usually a *turn the lights off and do it naked* type of gal."

"Kind of. Yeah."

"Does that mean you hate the idea?" He hovered his hand millimeters from her face, close enough for her to feel without him making contact.

She couldn't vocalize her concerns. "No. But..."

He cupped her cheek. "You weren't shy before."

"I didn't let myself think about it." Even though she lost the weight years ago, the doubt still lingered. Now was a horrid time for Danny's voice to echo in her head, which she suspected was why it did. This was an entirely different beast from picking up a stranger in a club. As much as she tried to convince herself otherwise, Jonathan's opinion meant the world to her.

"Then stop thinking now." He moved his hands to the bottom of her T-shirt. "I'll help." He peeled the top off, then grasped her hands as he looked her over. "Gorgeous."

The compliment and unwavering attention drilled inside, chasing away some of her hesitation, but not all. She hugged herself, unsure what to do next.

"Don't be that way." He loosened her arms again and stepped closer. Dropping his mouth to her ear, he whispered, "I want to see what you like. The way you caress yourself. The places you touch when you're alone with your thoughts. You show me yours; I'll show you mine."

He put distance between them but never stopped watching her. She forced boldness through her veins, letting her screaming pulse carry it, and unclasped her bra. It dropped to the ground, and the chill clashed with her scorched skin. "What now?"

"Up to you. For the number of times I fantasized about you... the reality is much better." His voice was heavy, a tone rapidly becoming her favorite.

She pushed the rest of her clothing to the ground. Her nipples were tight, and need throbbed between her legs. How was this such a turn-on? She'd worry about the why later. She preferred to focus on the now. She grabbed the chair from next to the desk and took a seat.

If she were alone… she'd hide under the covers and get things over with quickly.

That wasn't quite true. She imagined more, and now was her chance to make it real. When she dragged her thumbs over her nipples, he groaned.

That made this easier. Dampness grew between her legs. She pinched harder, rolling and squeezing. The touch made her gasp. She was tempted to fall into her own mind, but the sound of a zipper kept her in the room.

Jonathan undid his jeans and worked his cock free, gaze never leaving her. Her heart hammered in her chest. This was way hotter than she expected. She glided one hand down her stomach, still massaging her breast with the other. It never felt this good when she was alone.

She slid her fingers easily between her folds.

"God." Jonathan moaned. "Spread your legs. I want to see."

She complied, stroking along her slit, keeping away from her core, not wanting the experience to end too quickly.

"You made the most delicious sounds last night." Jonathan's voice was strained. "I want to hear them again. Those gasps and cries when you come."

She dipped two fingers inside her, thrusting and grinding against her hand. It wasn't enough. She moved back to her clit, and bucked against her touch when she nudged the swollen nub.

His grunts added to her urgency. She rubbed, as climax built inside. Edging. Getting closer. She pressed in, until orgasm spilled inside, tearing from her throat and making her body shudder.

"Jesus, Ale." His groan drew her attention again. He stroked his shaft, still watching her.

Inspiration struck, and she slid from the chair to kneel in front of him. "Want help?" She looked up at him through her lashes.

Not waiting for an answer, she trailed her tongue over the head of his cock, licking away a drop of precum. She took his length in her mouth. He was warm and hard, jerking against her, tangling his fingers in her hair to guide the pace.

His thrusting grew faster, and she licked along his skin. His groans shifted to frantic, seconds before a warm, salty squirt hit the back of her throat. She kept sucking until he wrenched from her touch, then she pulled away gently and met his gaze again.

He pulled her into his lap and kissed her deeply, not seeming to mind that his taste lingered on her lips. He broke away and pressed his forehead to hers. "So incredible," he said breathlessly.

Thunder clapped, and for a moment the entire room filled with the flash of lightning. Seconds later, the scramble of claws on hardwood drew closer, and a white flash of fur shot across the floor and under the dresser. The candle on top wobbled, then toppled onto the quilt draped over the rack next to it.

The blanket caught fire and sent flame shooting toward the ceiling and smoke billowing through the room. "*Shit.*" Jonathan was on his feet in an instant.

ELEVEN

JONATHAN YANKED THE BLANKET FROM THE WOODEN rack and tossed it to the floor. Sparks hit his bare skin, and a flaming chunk of stuffing landed on his hand, burning partway through his gauze before he could shake it off.

"Here." Bailey slid him the throw rug from next to the bed.

Within moments, he beat back the fire, until the quilt was nothing but a charred and melted shell in the middle of a scorch mark. Heavy smoke stung his eyes.

Bailey coughed until it sounded like she might evict a lung.

He wrapped an arm around her waist and guided them back downstairs.

They couldn't open the windows in this weather or turn on any fans without power, but at least most of the dense air stayed upstairs, and Lucifer had beaten a hasty retreat to the kitchen table. He looked Bailey over. Ash smudged her nose, her bare arms, and her stomach. He was probably an even bigger mess. Something about the thought drew a laugh from him, and once he started chuckling, he couldn't stop.

"Care to share with the group?" Bailey's voice was hoarse.

He dragged in a few deep breaths and swallowed the amusement. "I think—given the number of disasters in the last forty-eight hours that led to one or both of us being wet, burned, or covered in sludge—we may be better off spending the rest of my visit naked."

"I wouldn't complain"—she trailed her gaze over him with an attention that threatened to make him hard again—"but it's only fair if both of us are doing it."

He pulled her close again, wishing he had shed his clothes too. Marveling at the sensation of her soft body pressed against his, he kissed her forehead.

"I don't want to get splinters in my butt." She draped her arms around his neck.

"We're done in the attic, and all the other floors are polished. No worries there."

"One worry." She buried her face in his chest, muffling her voice. "You're distracting, and we're still on a schedule."

The schedule. Right. The same one that meant he was heading back home in less than a week. For the first time since arriving here, he wasn't in such a hurry to leave. The pressing desire to get back to the office was still there, but leaving Bailey behind...

Was exactly what he needed to do. It was a good reminder this entire thing was a means to close the door on his past. The house, the possessions, the fun with Bailey—he needed to enjoy it now, because it wasn't his to keep. In a week he'd be back in L.A., she'd stay here, and life would return to what it should be. What it was always meant to be.

THE LIGHTS WERE STILL out the next morning. Bailey wasn't surprised. With mainland transportation cut off, and the horrific conditions, no one was worried about a little substation that serviced such a small population.

Not that she was complaining; the company was good. She snuggled back into Jonathan and pulled his arm more tightly around her. She slept well despite the lingering smell of smoke, and having him there made the couch feel comfortable. She didn't know if she was relieved or just a little disappointed they found their way into some clothes before falling asleep last night.

"Morning." He moved his lips against her hair.

"Hey."

"What's on the schedule today, boss?"

She smiled, though he couldn't see it. "I hadn't thought past right now."

He moved his hand to her hip and nudged up the edge of her T-shirt, enough to touch bare skin. "I'm not going to push the issue, then. I'm fine with this."

"We have to get up eventually."

"Do we?"

"Yes." She laughed. This was perfect. Which sucked, because it would end soon.

It was better that way. With him gone, she could get him out of her system, have a clear head to remember why she didn't do long-term relationships, and go back to building a business he didn't approve of because it wouldn't make a lot of money. "Do you like living in L.A.?" She frowned at her own question, unsure where it came from.

"I never thought about it. It's familiar. It's also smoggy, overcrowded, hot and muggy, and never rains." As he talked, he traced her waist with his thumb. It was as comforting and familiar as it was seductive.

"If that's on the travel brochure, they need a better tourism department. It sounds miserable."

His quiet chuckle rumbled through her back. "Actually, I love it. A lot of people don't, and others think it's all big stars and homeless people, with nothing in between. I picked it though, and I don't regret it. I enjoy the big-city feeling. My office is close to home, which means I usually walk to work, and there's so much culture. So much to do and see. After all these years, it hasn't gotten old."

Like Atlanta, but bigger. "It sounds amazing."

"You think so?" He sounded surprised.

She didn't expect that reaction. "Why wouldn't I?"

"Well… You know." Vague and obscure, even by his terms.

She shifted her weight, to glance over her shoulder and look at him. "I don't have any idea, but I'm curious."

He pulled back, so she could lie down and see him. He moved his hand to her stomach. "I watch a lot of movies, as you know. And they've all told me —because really, we should trust what movies teach us—that the small-town girl always wants to stay in the small town. If she leaves, and especially if she gets a taste of the big city, when it's all over she wants to be back where there are as many cows as people."

"We don't have cows here."

"You know what I mean." He tickled her until she squealed and grabbed his hand, then returned to the light touch above her waist.

"If I thought for a second you believed everything you saw on TV, we wouldn't be cuddling."

Cuddling. She liked the way the word rolled off her tongue. "I stay here because it's financially convenient. I've thought about moving to Atlanta, but…"

"But what?"

She was going to say too much held her here. That wasn't right, though. Her memories were tied to the people, not the place, and there were as many bad ones as good. Besides, all those people were gone. "I guess I can't put it into words."

"You don't have to." He dipped his head, to brush his lips over hers.

Each time he did that, she wondered at how natural it felt. Both the kisses and the tender touches. Anything intimate that he didn't hesitate to do. Not a good place for her to dwell. "You really compared other women to me in college?" she asked.

"I did tell you that, didn't I?" His smile turned sheepish. "That night we kissed was a defining point in my life. So much changed."

Everything changed. She got engaged. He left and swore he'd never be back. "Yet you still walked away and let me go through with it." She snapped her jaw shut. Stupid bitter thoughts were supposed to stay in her head.

He sat up, and the chill that rushed in around her was from more than the suddenly missing body heat. His face slid into its impassive mask. "After I begged and pleaded with you to tell Danny *no*, I didn't want to see that happen. Especially with the way things ended up, but even before I knew." The words should be passionate and moving, but his flat delivery destroyed their impact.

She could do the same. Keep her emotion under control and pretend she hadn't reopened a gaping wound. "*Begged and pleaded* is a bit severe." She extracted herself from the couch and took a spot in the chair across from him.

"No. It's not." The edge snapped into his voice and was gone as quickly. "I told you he wasn't faithful."

"It was an open relationship." The retort slipped out, without her having to grab for it. The excuse that kept her by Danny's side for years, even after they closed things up.

"That you didn't want to be open. And who goes from *let's date the rest of the world at the same time* to *I love you. Marry me*? And who does that when they're eighteen?"

Dating more than one person or getting married? She wasn't sure she wanted his answer. "At least he told me how he felt." Fuck this. She wasn't staying calm. The hurt spilling into her words wouldn't let her. "He might have been deranged and screwed up and not had any idea what the words meant, but *he* had the balls to say something."

Jonathan glared at her and drew his lips into a straight line. "I would have done anything to stop you from making that mistake. I don't do regrets, yet I'd go back in a heartbeat and take you away from that. I did everything I could think of at the time. What else was I supposed to do?"

"Tell me you loved me."

JONATHAN DID his best not to get pissed off about the conversation, at the same time wondering how they went from sweet to snippy in a blink.

Her last words, as simple as they were, pushed him past his limits. "I wasn't going to tell you that." He couldn't keep the irritation hidden anymore. "I mean, I was ready to, before I found out about Danny. But I wasn't willing to manipulate you like that. *No. Don't marry him. I love you.* It had to be your own decision." He hadn't meant to put the confession out there. Did she notice?

"It's not manipulative if it's true, and that logic didn't stop you from sticking your tongue down my throat."

"That kiss went both ways. You fucking kissed me back. Do you really believe Danny ever thought he was lying to you? Each time he warped your mind with misdirection and cruel fucking lies—" He snapped the words off when her expression twisted from a scowl to a grimace. He crossed the room. "I shouldn't have brought that up."

"Why not? You made your point." She crossed her arms.

He was tired of wondering what transgression or misstep he'd commit next, to destroy the peace and fun they discovered. "Is that why you didn't want to see me again? You blame me for what happened? It's my fault you got married?"

"No."

"Are you sure?"

TWELVE

Was Bailey blaming Jonathan? She absolutely was, but admitting it out loud made it sound even pettier than in her head. He'd meant to say he loved her, way back when? That had her reeling. So many mistakes. So many wasted years.

It didn't matter? He still would have left for college, and everything else would be the same..?

"Bailey?" His irritation was almost tangible.

She didn't like that. "Yes."

"Yes... what? You're sure you're not blaming me?"

"No. I am. And maybe I shouldn't be—because you're right; it was my decision—but that doesn't stop me from feeling like you had something to do with it. You were right there. You only had to say one thing, and you *wanted* to say it." Her frustration was turning to tears, and she didn't want that.

"You could have *asked*. I didn't know what you wanted. Guess what? Not a fucking mind reader. You can't put this on me, because I'm not the only one who kept their mouth shut."

"But you saw things I didn't." This was ridiculous and childish, and that didn't stop her from feeling that way. Now was her chance to get it all out.

"And I tried to point them out to you." His voice rose in volume, and he winced. "Fine. Let's do this your way. Let's dive back into the past and pretend things went different, though we can't fucking change anything. I said, *No, Bailey. Don't marry him. I love you more.* And you said, *Oh, really? Me too.*"

The words she would have given anything for then sounded harsh and cold now. She wanted him to take it back. "Don't do this."

"Do what? Face reality? I just want one more minute. Then we're done. How does it go from there? I leave for college; that was the plan. I'd ask if you wanted to be my girlfriend. We'd date long distance. But it didn't have to play out that way. You could join me. Go to UC Berkeley. Except it's not that easy. You'd have to wait a year to start, because you hadn't applied yet, and you might as stay here and save up. That's what you tell me. Email makes it easy to stay in touch, but I'm *so* far away.

"And then the next asshole comes along, and I haven't said *I love you* nearly enough, because I'm on the other side of the fucking country and college is hard. So one day, your message to me says, *It's over. I'm marrying Billy Bob.* Which still brings us back to where we are, and it's still not my fucking fault you exercised poor judgment."

She didn't know if the fake past made her more hurt or furious. "Now I know how you really feel about my ability to think for myself."

"That's not me. That's *you*. If it's my fault you made shitty decisions, that never changes. I'm sorry life sucked with Danny. No one deserves that, and I'd give anything for you to not have gone through it, but I can't change the decisions I made. I thought I was doing the right thing. The same way you did."

"No one's to blame, then. Fantastic." She stood and brushed past him. "Conversation's over. Life goes on."

He grabbed her arm. "It's not over, because you're still pissed off, and nothing's been resolved."

"Sometimes things don't get fixed." She forced herself to meet his gaze and wrenched herself free from his grip. "But I've got a solution. We get back to work. As soon as the roads open, you go home and we never speak again. That's how this plays out, right? Because I'm so bad at making up my mind, and you sure as hell don't want to be here. So we pretend to gloss this over, according to your magical powers of perception, and it still aches inside and we never really forgive or forget. I'll still be fickle, and you'll still be a callous asshole who loves numbers more than people."

None of the words sounded right in her head, but she was too hurt and angry to take them back. Now the things she tried to convince herself she didn't mean were on the table. When it came down to it, she did mean them.

He didn't adopt that stupid blank mask of his. One thing to be grateful for. Instead, hurt and fury reflected back at her from his dark eyes. "Sounds perfect. How about that? We agree after all." Hard lines creased his forehead, and he spoke through clenched teeth. "I'll be in my room, throwing things out. You do… whatever it is you do."

She had to clench her jaw, to keep from saying anything else when he stepped around her. She couldn't spit out an apology, because everything was too raw for her to mean it. If she opened her mouth, more half-thought-out notions would slip out. Things that weren't true, but parts of her held onto with ferocity. She no longer had to worry about it aching when they parted ways. The pain could start now, and be a numb throb in a few days.

JONATHAN STRUGGLED to find reason through the haze of anger clouding his thoughts. This was worse than being drunk. It was also a fantastic reminder of why he let work take priority over personal relationships. He made his way into the kitchen and grabbed a handful of trash bags. When Bailey's soft, gasping sob landed against his back, he refused to look.

That entire conversation was a mistake. He got sucked in, he said things he didn't mean, and he let it cut deep. Worse, he watched the words devour her and didn't take any of it back.

He strode up the stairs without looking in her direction, and cut a line for his old room.

Gray light peeked around the edges of his windows, but between the shutters, the storm, and the lingering smoke, it was hard to see. He didn't care. Most of this was junk. He'd scrape it into bags, and set it out with the rest of the garbage.

The plastic dinosaurs went first, followed by the army of green soldiers guarding a model car. He grabbed the car to sweep it into the bag, and hesitated. The toys were almost all gifts from his parents and friends of the family. Things they insisted little boys needed, growing up. He had to be the weird kid and ask for a scientific calculator when he was nine. He got the model car kit instead.

The memory added another layer of pain to what simmered inside. He'd sat up here, whining about how much he hated the stupid thing. Bailey argued it was awesome and pulled the parts from their box. The cheap pieces didn't fit together the way she wanted. She was ready to give up on it too, until he pointed out where they had to sand and what parts needed a touch of heat to warp them and make it all click.

The red paint glopped in places and left plastic exposed on others, but back then they were so proud of it.

This was why he didn't want to come back here. He set the model in its home, to be dealt with later, and turned his attention to the closet. Nothing hung from the bar. His clothes had come and gone with him each year. As he grew older, he got snobby. Refused to wear anything that wasn't trendy. The memories of teenage-him would make him laugh if they didn't carry so much else.

He used his phone as a flashlight. The battery would be dead by the end of the day, unless the power came back on, but without a signal, it didn't matter.

Boxes were stacked high. He grabbed the first one and grunted when he realized how heavy it was. A peek inside showed books about mathematical theories, patterns, and code breaking. This was all his stuff. He set it aside. They were old and so out of date they weren't useful anymore, but they could be donated.

The remainder of the boxes were the same. Sorting through them didn't take as long as he hoped, and all he did was shift the stack from the closet to the edge of the room. He might have to go back to the toys on the shelf sooner than he expected.

A twinge of pain shot through his right hand, and he dropped his phone out of reflex. "Fuck." He wiggled his fingers, to get rid of the ache, and knelt to retrieve the device. *Don't let it be cracked.* It was fine, as far as he could tell. Maybe scratched but still usable. The light cast along the back wall, reflecting a shine.

"What the...?" He tried to angle himself better, to get another look, but couldn't find whatever caught his eye. He was about to give up, when he caught the glint again. He crawled into the closet and ran his fingers along the wooden paneling, until he hit a bump. A latch? No. Couldn't be. It didn't matter how many stories Nana told, or if they had a toe in reality; she didn't have hidden compartments around her house.

The logic didn't stop him from fiddling with the metal clasp. Did it twist? Push? Flip up?

He heard a soft *click*, and a musty smell wafted into the room, to blend with the lingering smoke. Sure enough, an entire panel of the wall was offset from the rest now. Curiosity blanketed his bleak thoughts. He scooted back to pull the door open, and found a safe inside.

The digital keypad indicated it hadn't been

there for centuries or even decades. It had to be fairly new.

He pocketed his phone, tugged the small box from its hidden spot, and carried it to the bed, where the light was better. How was he supposed to open it? He drummed his fingers on his leg, cycling through a list of possible number combinations. He could start with something simple, like a series of six 1's and work his way up the list, but that would take ages. So what numbers mattered to her? He tried combinations of her social security number, the address here, his dad's birthday... He racked his brain for stories she'd told him and any significant numbers therein.

Something nudged the back of his thoughts, and he couldn't quite grasp it. The idea was simple, but he didn't know why Nana would go with it. It wouldn't work, but maybe trying it would knock another idea loose. He typed in 1-6-6-9-8-6. January 6 and June 9, 1986. His and Bailey's birthdays.

A soft series of beeps flitted through the room, and the safe clicked open. *Damn that woman.* The thought only held fondness. A cardboard box in plastic sat inside. He extracted it and unwrapped it carefully, anticipation growing.

Photos sat inside. Not like those in the album downstairs. These were yellowed and faded with age, and Nana was in them, a much younger woman than Jonathan ever knew. Probably in her late teens or early twenties. In some of the pictures she was with an older man. A grandfather? That wasn't right. Nana loved her photos, and Jonathan had seen dozens of his family dating back several generations. The man was familiar, but not family. Jonathan couldn't place where he'd seen him before.

He sifted through more of the shots. When he reached one of his grandmother lying across a fainting couch in practically nothing, he coughed in shock and dropped the stack. He moved it aside to reveal the next, with her wearing even less.

"Jesus." He didn't know if he was more disturbed or amused. He'd stumbled on naughty photos of Nana. Either way, he wasn't interested in looking at more.

At the bottom of the box sat a film reel. Interesting. She had a projector upstairs. A nagging voice asked if he really wanted to see the movie, given what was else was in the box. *Maybe later.* He gathered it all up and was about to set it back in the safe, when something else caught his eye. An envelope with his name on it, in Nana's flowing scrawl.

A loud crash shook the house. It wasn't the storm; it came from beneath him. Louder than boxes falling. "*Bailey?*" he shouted.

A whisper of concern snaked through him when she didn't answer. It might be like the other day, and she was fine. Had she always been so accident prone? He couldn't shake the worry. He sprinted down two flights of stairs, not slowing until he hit the ankle-deep water in the basement.

Light shone at the far end of the room, illuminating the concrete wall but not much else between him and it. "Bailey?" As his eyes adjusted to the darkness, he made out dark shadows that looked like fallen shelves. The water was only a couple inches deep. He picked his way across the room, trying to avoid stepping on anything. He should have worn shoes. He didn't see any movement in the room besides his own shadow. He reached the fallen shelves, and his heart dropped into his stomach when he found a warm body pinned underneath. A cinderblock sat on one of Bailey's arms, and a dark gash glared across her forehead.

Fear pushed aside any of his anger from earlier. Her chest rose and fell. That was a good sign. He shifted everything off her. Her arm sat at an awkward angle. "*Fuck.*" He pressed a hand to her forehead and pulled it away. Dark, sticky blood covered his skin. He didn't dare move her without knowing the extent of her injuries, and he was terrified to leave her alone while she was unconscious.

He could take her to a doctor. If the clinic was open. If it wasn't, he had no idea where the current practitioner lived. "Come on, Ale." He brushed the hair off her face. "Please?"

THIRTEEN

BAILEY'S HEAD HURT MORE THAN SHE EVER remembered it hurting. She couldn't remember much, though. Her arm ached too. Why? She was fighting with Jonathan. Was this some kind of psychological reaction? It was dark. The power was still out. No, her eyes were closed. She struggled to force them open, and her skull protested.

The fighting wasn't the last thing she did. She'd been downstairs. Pissed because the basement flooded. Angry at Jonathan, for choosing now of all times to show emotion. Yanking stuff down in a frustrated rage. And then—

She reached for the *what next*, and her head screamed *no*.

A soft and warm sensation scuttled over her cheek. Bugs? The thought made her skin crawl. Lucifer? No. A hand.

"Wake up?" That was Jonathan. He didn't *sound* mad.

She tried again to open her eyes, and this time they responded. Dark shadows stood out amid lighter ones, and a silhouette hovered over her.

"Thank God." Jonathan sighed.

Something dabbed against her forehead, and she tried to reach up, to see what it was. When she lifted her arm, a whole new world of hurt greeted her, and she cried out.

"Careful." He helped her lower the arm back to the ground. "It's broken. And your head is bleeding."

A washcloth. That's what the sensation was. He held pressure against her skin. "You weren't out for long." He sounded worried. "Only a couple of minutes, but that's still not good." Did they make up?

Was that what she couldn't remember? "I'm okay." Why did she say that? Every inch of her protested when she tried to move. "No. I'm not."

"Can you tell if anything else is broken?" Even in the dim light, he looked concerned.

She shouldn't like that, but she did. She shifted, squirming on the floor, and forced herself to sit, favoring her arm the entire time. "I think the rest is okay."

"Good. You need a doctor. Odds the clinic is open?"

"Zero to less than none." She wanted to be valiant and argue she didn't need a doctor. To insist she'd be fine. The almost-useless appendage dangling by her side screamed loudly enough to convince her otherwise.

He helped her stand, and her world spun. "Slowly." He draped her good arm around his shoulders and steadied her, circling her waist and resting a hand on her hip. "Where does the doctor live?"

"Same place as always."

His chuckle was strained. "You're serious? He's got to be ninety now."

"It's only been a few years. He's in his sixties. But we can't go out in this weather." Whether or not she was in pain, some things were a bad idea. Now she wasn't lying in water, the chill of being soaked set in. She clenched her teeth, to keep them from chattering.

"Options. Stay here and ride out the storm. You've broken something and probably have a mild concussion, so that's not viable. With the gusting wind, walking is a stupid idea. Phones are down, so we can't call the guy, and even then, he'd have to get here. So you're getting in the car with me. We're risking the weather, to drive the one or two miles to his house, and we'll apologize profusely for imposing at his house, but he'll understand."

Now she remembered more about why they were fighting. "I hate it when you do that."

"Think things through?" He helped her up the stairs, not letting go until they reached the kitchen and she sat down.

"Yes. Freaking infuriating."

"At least your brain is working okay." He kissed her forehead. "Don't move." A moment later, he returned with a blanket, a sheet, her bag, and her shoes.

He tore the sheet into strips, and used one as a makeshift sling, to tie her arm to her torso. His every move was deliberate and gentle. Probably too much so, but she wasn't complaining. Next, he draped the blanket around her. Being wrapped up didn't chase away the chill completely, but it helped her stop shivering.

When they stepped outside, the wind slammed into her full force and sent another shock of pain from her arm and through her body. She stumbled, but Jonathan made sure she didn't fall. The drive to Dr. Phillips's house was two parts terrifying, as the car jostled with every gust from Mother Nature, and one part agonizing. Jonathan parked as close as the driveway let him, told her to wait, and sprinted to the door. Moments later, he returned with the doctor.

She lost track of what happened next. All she knew was she was finally warm and so tired.

MORE THAN FIFTEEN YEARS LATER, and Jonathan still hated this place. Not because of Dr. Phillips or anything wrong with the house. It was a lovely two-story Victorian-style home, with pleasant decor. There was even power in this room, thanks to a backup generator kept on hand for cases like this. The last time Jonathan visited was because he almost drowned during a storm a hell of a lot like the one going on now.

As far as he was concerned, his reason for being here today was a lot worse. He was assured Bailey would be fine. She drifted in and out of consciousness—a result of the painkillers pumping through her, and the mild concussion. Her arm was set and splinted without an issue, and though the doctor didn't have the equipment here to do a full head scan on her, she was responding all right. She just had to be careful until they could get her to a real hospital for a CT scan.

For now, Jonathan waited. He muddled through the sympathy about Nana's passing. Declined the offer to join Dr. and Mrs. Phillips for lunch. Hovered over Bailey in a way she'd hate if she realized.

Despite how recent their argument was, it felt stupid now. He didn't regret the things that came out, but his delivery could have used some work. He watched her now, as she slept. Why was it so hard for them to find common ground? They grew up— that changed them—but their friendship lingered. He wished it wasn't tainted by unshakable memories.

He jammed his hands into his pockets and frowned when the right one touched something. The envelope from the safe. He gave Bailey another glance—she was still sleeping—and tore the letter open.

A single sheet of paper sat inside, on the stationary Nana always used to write him, in her familiar scrawl. A lump formed in his throat when he saw it was dated the day before she died.

Jonathan,

I'm sorry I'll never see you again. I'm grateful you kept in touch.

Fate is a funny thing.

The sudden shift in subjects made him frown, but he kept reading.

It doesn't matter how hard you try to avoid it, it always finds you. Except in your case. You've dodged yours every step of the way.

I don't think anyone's future should be set in stone, but I hope you stop running sooner rather than later. That you pause long enough to see what's been right in front of you for so long.

I love you, and I couldn't be more proud of you. Never think otherwise.

Love,

Nana

He swallowed past the ache in his chest and stared at the handwritten note, trying to make sense of what she meant about fate. Why did the words nag at him?

Something rustled, and he shoved the letter in his pocket again. He looked up, to see Bailey blinking a couple of times before completely opening her eyes.

"Hey." Her smile looked like it took effort.

"How are you feeling?"

"Everything hurts, but not as much as it did."

He reached for her working hand and grasped her fingers. "Good drugs."

"I'll say. What time is it?"

"Almost six at night. You slept for a while."

She pushed herself into a sitting position, keeping her weight on her good arm. "I'll say. Phillips isn't going to make me stay all night, is he?"

"He said we couldn't leave until there was a break in the storm."

She looked down, and saw she wore a hospital gown. She frowned. "Where are my clothes?"

"Mrs. Phillips had to cut your shirt off, to get you into something dry, without jarring you too much. I hope it wasn't a favorite. She's washing your jeans."

Bailey sank back into her pillows with an *oof.* "It

sounds like a ruined top is the least of my concerns. And no, it wasn't a favorite."

"I'm sorry about earlier." He should wait to have this conversation, but the apology needed to be out there.

"No, you're not." She didn't look or sound upset. "We both said what we meant to."

He couldn't argue that. "But there were better ways to say it. I'm tired of arguing. I'm not going to yield if I disagree, but there's got to be a happy medium."

"In that case, I'm sorry too." She squeezed his hand. "And if you're gone in a few days, we won't argue anymore anyway."

"About that…" The words slipped out before he realized what he was saying. He had to analyze the rest of the thought and figure out if he wanted to head down that road.

She raised her brows in question.

He had to try. "Come back to L.A. with me." The suggestion was ludicrous, and wouldn't be taken back. The longer the idea lingered in his head, the more he liked it.

Her surprised exhale wasn't quite the response he wanted. "Wow. I… uh— *Wow.*"

"You said this morning you've considered a bigger city and that nothing's keeping you here."

"That's not quite how the conversation went."

She didn't look upset, but the hesitation wasn't what he wanted to hear.

"It's a plan in progress."

"My livelihood is here. My sales connections. My regular customers."

This was the point where he should concede and tell her he understood. "I'll help you get re-established."

"And then what? You don't agree with my business plan. What did you say? It wasn't the kind of thing that made money." Sadness lined her words.

"There are ways to improve on the idea. I can help." *Stop talking. Drop it.* He refused to listen to the voice in his head.

She tugged his fingers. "I don't want help with that." Her tone was calm and even. "I'm happy with the idea the way it is, and the gallery I want is here."

"You wanted to know earlier what could have been thirteen years ago. This is our chance to find out. Minus the sarcastic cynicism."

"The teenager in me wants to find out," she said. "She's so very desperate for me to say *yes*. But we don't know each other. I adore the boy I grew up with. I hope you feel the same, but—you know—the other way around. The problem is, we clash every time the real world rears its head. A lot of that's on me; I have so much baggage... You're the one who makes the predictions. How do you think this plays out? I'm guessing I give up my life here, sell every-thing, and move in with you. Sounds amazing. Until the fighting gets worse and the memories can't hold us together. Do I have that right?"

"Real close." He didn't want to concede, but she had a point. "The sex is amazing."

She smirked. "I can't argue that, but it doesn't make a relationship. Ask me again though, and I won't say *no*."

He was thinking clearly enough to know that would be a huge mistake. "I won't ask again. Get some rest until Phillips says we can go." He slumped back in his chair, trying to make sense of what just happened. The conversation felt backwards and nonsensical. Or rather, it should. Instead, the only part that confused him was where it ended with a *no*.

FOURTEEN

Bailey woke up to sunlight striking her face, and a screaming headache. A weight pressed against her hand, and she forced her head to the side. What she saw made her smile and temporarily erased the pain. Jonathan sat in a chair by her side, head resting on the bed. The clock on the far wall said it was almost eight. She assumed from the sunlight it was morning. Did the storm pass?

Jonathan stirred and looked up. His hair stuck up in every direction, pale stubble covered his chin, and he had a red mark on his cheek. He looked sexy as heck, and it reminded her of the conversation the night before.

He gave her a tired smile and scooted back to stretch. "How do you feel?"

"Like a cinderblock shelf fell on me." She forced a laugh.

"Are you two decent?" Dr. Phillips called, seconds before stepping into the doorway. "How do you feel?"

She'd already used her joke. "Like crap."

"To be expected." He strolled past Jonathan, fitting his glasses on as he walked, then pulled a mini-flashlight from his pocket. He held her eyes open and shone the bright light in one and then the other. He tapped, poked, and tested her responses to various stimuli. "The storm broke a few hours ago. As long as you're up for it, you can go home. But you can't be alone for the next twenty-four hours. Will that be an issue?"

Last night she would have said *it'll be fine* in a heartbeat. Now she wasn't sure where she and Jonathan stood.

"Not an issue." Jonathan spoke up.

Dr. Phillips didn't look surprised. "As long as the weather is calm tomorrow morning, I want you in my office… God willing, it's still standing. Until we can get you to the hospital, I want to do an X-ray and make sure everything is where it should be. Both the arm and the head. No driving yourself, and he has to wake you up every few hours to make sure you're responding."

"Yes, sir," she said.

"Good. Take your time getting up. No standing quickly. No heavy exertion." He glanced at Jonathan, and Bailey's cheeks heated. "Be careful."

An hour later, Phillips cleared her to leave. Mrs. Phillips loaned Bailey a tank-top that could be pulled on around the cast without too much effort. A small thing to be grateful for, but Bailey would take whatever she could find.

The room spun when Bailey sat up and then stood, but it righted itself quickly. There was nothing sexual about the way Jonathan helped her into the top. He cradled her arm, ensuring it wasn't jarred, and when he tugged down the hem, he glided his fingers over her skin with a tenderness she wasn't used to when he tugged the hem down.

On the way out, Mrs. Phillips handed Jonathan a paper bag that looked weighed down. She told him it was leftovers and to make sure both of them ate. She pulled Bailey aside while he took things out to the car. "I'm so happy to see the two of you together. You deserve it."

The simple comment, as well intentioned as it might be, sent a cascade of emotion to clutter the inside of Bailey's head. She didn't have the strength to correct the older woman, so she simply smiled and thanked her for the hospitality.

Bailey fell into her own thoughts on the short drive back to Nana's, and stayed there as she and Jonathan made their way inside. He got her settled on the couch and opened a couple upstairs' windows, to clear out the lingering smoke.

Jack and Ale. Up until the point Bailey got engaged to Danny, everyone here assumed she'd end up with Jonathan. Sometimes it was embarrassing, but mostly younger-her loved it and fell into the same fantasy. Now the presumption nagged at her. It was one of the things she both loved and hated about living in such a close-knit community—everyone knew everyone else's business and that certain things would happen, because people expected them to.

No one here knew Jonathan anymore, but he'd been a nice boy, and heaven forbid she stay single. The bitter thought bothered her. Or maybe what sat at the heart of it all disturbed her more than anything. His offer echoed over the questions and doubt. It was sweet, despite being misguided. Turning him down was the right thing to do, and once she convinced all of herself, this muddled mess would clear up.

"You want lunch?" Jonathan's question carried from the kitchen.

Her stomach growled. Had it really been more than a day since she last ate? The last twenty-four hours seemed as though they lasted an eternity. "Yes."

Moments later, he handed her a plate with pasta salad and fresh vegetables. "Note to self." He settled into the overstuffed easy chair. "Always visit the house with a backup generator when we forget to stock up for a big storm. I mean—" His head shot up.

"I know what you mean." *Hello, awkwardness.*

Most of the meal passed in silence, interrupted by Jonathan telling her he'd finish the clean-up work and sorting. She had to tell him what was worth auctioning when he asked. He cleared away the lunch dishes, and she made her way upstairs. The sky was graying again. There was a good chance they'd ridden out the eye of the storm and were in for Round Two tonight. They'd have to shutter the windows again soon, just in case.

She locked herself in the bathroom and let the silence and solitude wash over her. Pale light bled in through the window—enough to see without power. She let the water run until the cold stung her hand and numbed her skin, then splashed her face. The chill gave her something external to focus on and drew her out of her thoughts. It was getting crowded in her head. She looked up, and her reflection stared back. Bleary eyed, with messy hair and the hard lines of a frown etched everywhere.

If she looked into her own eyes long enough, would she find answers or simply get lost? She flung the cabinet door open in frustration, not wanting to see the image. Three shelves greeted her. This was better. Boxes of bandages and bottles of vitamins, allergy medicine, and acid reducers didn't care if she was indecisive.

The cabinet would need to be cleared, and most of this could be thrown out. She grabbed the plastic trashcan from the floor, set it on the counter, and began to fill it. She pulled the items from their shelves one by one, liking the simplicity of the action.

When she reached an empty prescription bottle, she paused. Nana never threw away memories, but an empty bottle was a different story. Bailey frowned when she saw the prescription name on the bottle, for the same painkiller Dr. Phillips gave her this morning. Where Bailey only had five pills—enough to hold her over until they could do more tests—this said it was for fifty. She never realized Nana suffered that kind of pain.

Bailey's curiosity and confusion grew when she saw the date on the bottle. Written and filled less than two weeks ago. She struggled to match the information to the time she'd spent with Nana, as she set aside the bottle and moved to the next. It was half full. A drug Bailey didn't recognize. Or did she? The name tickled her thoughts, but she couldn't grasp the association. Whatever it was, Nana had been taking it a lot longer. The bottle had three refills left, and the prescription was written ten months ago.

She set the two orange bottles aside and continued her cabinet cleaning, letting the question roll around in the back of her head. It was a much better place for her focus than trying to figure out what to do about Jonathan.

When the pieces clicked, she frowned. She knew the drug name because Margaret mentioned it one day, when Bailey was at the art gallery. It was a new Alzheimer's drug Margaret's father was on. But Nana didn't have…

Crap. More of the picture formed in Bailey's head. The lapses in memory that started to show over the last few years. Nana asking where Jonathan was, then laughing it off later as a joke. Prodding Bailey about her marriage, then shaking it away as a lingering concern. There was more, too, but Bailey couldn't wrap her brain around how the two bottles were connected. What were the odds Dr. Phillips would give her information during her visit tomorrow? Nonexistent, most likely. It wouldn't stop her from trying.

She filed away the questions for later and opened the bathroom door. She came up short when she almost ran into Jonathan.

"You all right?" He searched her face. "You look pale."

"Other than the concussion? I'm fine." She stopped short of telling him what she found. The knowledge wouldn't change anything, and she didn't know what she'd say. *I think Nana had Alzheimer's and never told anyone.* It felt like there would be more to that conversation. The statement felt incomplete.

The microwave beeped, and lights flickered on around the house. She was grateful for the distraction. A twisting in her gut asked if she should dig deeper into the pill question. She didn't want to, but she needed the whole story.

JONATHAN STARED at the attic in frustration. With everything reorganized, it was easy to tell what types of things were where, but he wanted a specific item. He poked his head through the trap door. "*Bailey.*"

"Yeah?" She'd grumbled about being mostly confined to the couch, but acquiesced when she figured out it gave her an excuse to make lists of the auction items they uncovered.

Having the power back on made it easier to get through the outstanding work. Especially since an awkward silence hovered in the air every time he and Bailey were in the same room. He didn't regret making his offer last night, but it changed things. Where did it leave them? Friends? Nothing?

"Did you come across that old movie projector?" The note he found in the bottom of the safe sat in his wallet now, not offering more answers than when he first read it. He could decipher one riddle, though—what was on the film reel under the old photos.

"*To-sell* stack. Probably on the bottom."

That gave him what he needed. Moments later, he unearthed the gray box and hauled it from the pile. Something else tumbled to the ground, and he frowned. A small, velvet jewelry box. He flipped the top, to expose a gold ring, inlaid with diamonds and engraved with delicate leaves. He recognized it. It was Nana's mother's wedding ring. An heirloom, passed down for generations. He was glad it wasn't lost.

He pocketed the box and hefted the projector down the ladder. He paused in his room to grab the film, and then made his way to the living room.

Bailey looked up from her notes. "What's that?" Before he could respond, she added, "Besides a projector."

He raised his brows, entertained. "I found a movie. I want to see what's on it."

"Government secrets?" Her words were playful.

He dragged the coffee table to a spot close to an outlet but far enough from the blank wall on the far side of the room, that the image would show up. "My money's on deleted scenes from Gone with the Wind."

"Original director's cut of Casablanca?"

"Shirley Temple auditions." He almost expected one or all of the above. Or hoped for it. With all of Nana's stories about her adventures when she was younger, it would be amazing if the film was something rare and fantastic. He plugged the projector in, loaded the reels, and dimmed the lights. "Ready to watch history... of some sort?"

"Bring it on." Bailey laughed.

He flicked the switch. Crackles filtered through the ancient speakers—not caused by sound from the movie, but by the age of the film and player—and a sepia image covered the wall. It was Nana, looking identical to the woman in the photos upstairs. Fortunately this moving version was fully clothed.

"Wow." Awe filled Bailey's voice. "Is that really her?"

"Yes."

"In that case, better than all of the above."

He agreed. There was no sound, as the woman on the wall moved about. The room she stood in was familiar, but he couldn't place it. It wasn't any of the houses around here, that he remembered. A man strolled into the frame. The same older gentleman as in the pictures.

"Is that Papa Hemingway?" Bailey's question flipped a switch in Jonathan's head.

"I think it is." That was why he looked familiar, as did the room. Ernest Hemingway's historic estate sat on one of the other Keys. The home of the American poet was a tourist attraction now. It all rushed back—Nana's tales about her torrid affair with the much older man; how she used to tease Jonathan's dad about being an illegitimate child; the way she insisted Hemingway killed himself. *Accident, cleaning his gun—my ass*, she'd say. *He knew he'd seen the best of life and wanted to go out on a high note.*

On screen, the man approached Nana. Jonathan almost choked, when Hemingway swept her into an embrace and kissed her passionately. Nana cupped the man's crotch, and Jonathan muttered, "Oh, God." Her partner tore her dress from her shoulders and groped her breast, and Jonathan flipped off the projector. "Nope. We're done." Historic documents were one thing, but there was no way he was watching his grandmother in some sort of late-forties amateur porn movie.

"Holy…" Bailey trailed off. "That wasn't real. There's no way."

"I'd like to agree."

"Can you imagine how much that's worth if you can prove it's legit?"

Jonathan glared at her, and she held up her hands. "Teasing. Seriously. Where did you find it?"

In the closet of shattered childhood delusions. He kept the sarcastic thought to himself. "In a safe upstairs." He stalled on the part about the note for him, and wasn't sure why. Maybe because, if Nana left the letter there, she intended for him to discover all of this.

"Do you think… That is… Were her stories about your real grandfather true?"

"No." He shook his head until his brain rattled. "Those were to fluster Dad; I'm not the illegitimate grandson of…" He couldn't say the name. It felt like sacrilege.

She sank back into the cushions. "How many more of her tales do you think are real? If this one happened, all bets are off."

"I'm going to go with all of them at this point." He dropped to the other end of the couch. Bailey shifted her legs to make room for him, then rested her feet on his thighs. "Hell. I think I want that treasure map and to go check out the far end of the island, to see what that iron key belongs to." He was being facetious. It was easier than processing the awe and disbelief. His entire life he thought he knew the woman who raised him, but apparently he had no idea.

She meant the world to him. Gave him more support and affection than his own parents. For as long as he remembered, her existence seemed to revolve around him, and he took that for granted. Yet, before he came along, before his father, she'd lived a rich life.

Ernest-Fucking-Hemingway, for God's sake. An author—an artist—who influenced the world. Jonathan struggled to reconcile the sweet old woman who led him on fake treasure hunts with the vibrant young girl in the movie looking up adoringly at her lover.

She'd *lived*. What was he doing with his life as a *thank you* for the time she gave him? Working. Earning. Ignoring anything inside that threatened to hurt. Was there something to her letter? Not that he thought he was running from fate, but was he letting life pass him by?

For the first time since hearing about her death, joyful memories of her flitted in without the grief. He wanted to hang onto this feeling for as long as he could.

FIFTEEN

"You're sure you don't want to sell the movie? Classic pornography with a famous leading man has to be worth a fortune to the right collector."

Jonathan stared at Bailey in disbelief, waiting for her to crack. She looked back impassively. He finally said, "With my *grandmother*."

She laughed. "Ow." She pressed her hand to her forehead.

"That's what you get." He kept his tone kind.

"Yeah, yeah. That won't stop me from doing it again."

"Teasing me? Wouldn't have it any other way."

She massaged her temple a bit more, before dropping her hand back to her lap. "I'm sorry about the other morning. Yesterday? I guess it was only a day ago."

"Don't worry about it." He was still wrapping

his head around the old movie—not just the contents, but all the thoughts it knocked loose. How much Nana and her stories meant. How she was there for Bailey when he wasn't. That he missed her so much it hurt in his chest and joints and every inch of his frame.

"I'm not dropping this until I've said what I need to. It can't fester when you leave. I won't let it be like last time."

He didn't have an argument. "I'm listening."

"I don't want to take back what I said." She frowned. "Well, I do, but it would be dishonest. I want to take back that I meant it, but I can't. It's not true anymore. I've blamed you forever for what happened, though I shouldn't have. In a way, I'm glad it happened like this."

He must have misunderstood. "How could you possibly be glad about it?"

"I don't like my time with Danny. That freaking hurt, and it came close to destroying me. But I came out the other side, and I like to think I'm better for it. I don't want you to hang onto it either."

"Already over it." He struggled to keep the teasing in his voice amid the chaos of emotion inside.

She chucked a throw pillow at him. "Bozo."

He snagged it from the air and set it on the ground. Lucifer crawled out from under the couch and climbed onto the plush. She turned around twice before lying down. "Have you been watching her since…" *Nana passed.* He couldn't say the words.

"I leave food out for her and clean her litter box. She hid until you got here. Thank you for putting food out for her while I was out of it."

"Will you take care of her once I leave?"

"Of course."

He managed to grab one of the many thoughts flitting around and force words to it. "I'm not as forgiving as you. If I saw Danny, I'd still deck him without hesitation."

"And I'd enjoy seeing it. Have you ever punched someone? Doesn't that dirty the suit?"

He was wrong before; Bailey wasn't three separate people. Teenage-her, bitter-adult-her, and the teasing seductive siren were all the girl he grew up with, and he'd missed her a lot. "It probably would, but you're worth the dry-cleaning bill."

"You're such a hero." She looked around. "Dang it. The cat stole my projectile weapon."

It felt good to laugh. It didn't erase the heaviness from his heart, but it sweetened the sadness. "I'm going to miss you."

"You don't have to."

He couldn't decipher her meaning. "I don't?"

"You know how to email. I'm half-surprised you didn't charge your phone the minute we got power. Either one of us is capable of hopping a plane. You don't have to drop off the face of the earth again."

"I won't. I promise. And I *am* sorry for the things I said yesterday."

She raised her brows in question.

"My made-up past for us. I don't think it would have gone down that way." Not that he could predict things like *what if* when it came to people. If she were a stock, he could guess to the penny. "But neither of us would be who we are now, and we're pretty fucking awesome as we are."

"Cornball." As if agreeing with her, thunder crashed outside and lightning lit the room, before the lights blinked out.

"I'll get the flashlights." He was reluctant to move. Sitting with her feet in his lap, simply talking, felt right.

"It'll wait. Tell me more about what Mr. Freaking Awesome does with his life."

This was the way it should be. They had their friendship back and wouldn't surrender it even with a country between them. He'd go back to work, she'd do the same, and somewhere along the way, they'd be happy for each other when they found the loves of their lives.

The idea wrenched in his stomach, and he swallowed his response.

THE STORM BLEW out by the next morning, and by ten, they had power again. Bailey resisted the urge to tease Jonathan about plugging in his phone within minutes of having lights, but she did get in a jab when he grumbled about still not having any service. He was treating her like a china doll, watching most of her movements and asking every few minutes how she was. He let her get up and walk around, as long as she promised not to do anything that would jar her broken arm. Which meant ignoring most of what she needed to do.

When a loud ring carried through the house, it took her a moment to place it. The phone.

"Got it." Jonathan slid past her and grabbed the handset. "Hello. She is…?" He was silent for almost a minute. "I see. Is everyone—? I'm glad. I'll let her know. This afternoon works. See you then." He hung up and looked at her. "No clue why Phillips thought to look for you here."

Because the town thinks we're a couple now that you're back. She didn't need to delve into that. She and Jonathan had their footing and friendship again. No reason to disrupt a good thing, and she was grateful for the peace they'd reached. "He knows I'm working on the estate. And you did bring me in."

"He says his clinic is up and running, and he wants to see you today for that X-ray."

"What else did he say?" There might not have been more, but Bailey had a haunting feeling that churned inside and made her wonder if she wanted the answer.

He turned his gaze to his feet and worked his jaw up and down before finally looking at her. "There was a fire downtown when the power came on last night. They think the wind blew branches into exposed electrical and sparks went up…"

"Is everyone all right?" Her looming dread crept in further.

"No one was hurt. They got it before it spread through all of Main Street, and put it out before the wind picked up again." He clenched his fist, then jammed his hand into his pocket.

"And…?"

He furrowed his brow. "I'm sorry."

"For what?" She didn't like this. Did he realize dragging things out made it worse?

"The fire started in Margaret's gallery. The prints, photos, paintings in oil… Phillips says it lit up like a pile of tinder. But she's all right. She left for the mainland before they closed the roads."

"That's something." Bailey's head spun, and she leaned against the wall for support.

"I know you were— You would have done a good job with the place, I'm sorry it's gone."

She forced herself to stand. "Nothing to do about it." She didn't believe her words. "I'll be fine. We need to get to the doctor, right?"

They kept up a steady string of conversation—

or rather, Jonathan did most of the talking—on the drive into town. She was grateful he didn't bring up the gallery again. It wasn't as though she'd lost something that was hers, and she was grateful no one was hurt, but she needed to process losing that dream, and she wasn't sure how to cope.

The clinic's waiting room was packed to the point of standing room only with people with sniffles, coughs, and minor injuries they'd held onto through the hurricane. Bailey chatted with all of them and refused to acknowledge the knowing looks they shot Jonathan. She was grateful for the reprieve when she was shown back to a room. Even waiting another thirty minutes to see the doctor didn't bother her. It was a chance to be alone with her musings.

While she never thought she could find the funds to buy the gallery, that hadn't stopped her from hoping. The loss wouldn't wreck her business, which followed the estate sales. She'd still spend her weekends in Georgia and marvel at the antiques and memories people collected without realizing they did it.

The nurse made small talk while they X-rayed Bailey's skull, then left the room again. Moments later, Dr. Phillips joined her and pinned the slides to the lightbox on the wall.

"You're looking good." He pointed at the black

and white image. "On the surface, there are no cracks. How are you feeling?"

Physically? Fine. Mentally, tired of the question. "Arm hurts, but the dizziness is gone."

"Glad to hear it." He flipped off the light beneath the images. "I don't think you'll have any long-term damage, but I want to know the minute you have any issues with things like balance or memory."

Issues with memory. A thought was triggered in her head, and she failed to grasp it. "Can I ask you something?"

"Certainly."

"Did Nancy Woodhouse have any issues with her memory?"

Dr. Phillips let out a breath as if he'd been socked in the gut, and turned away from her. He pulled off his glasses and polished them with the hem of his scrubs top. "Why do you ask?"

"I found two prescriptions in the medicine cabinet."

"*You* did."

She didn't like the evasion. Did no one in this town know how to give a straight answer? "Yes."

"I'm grateful it wasn't Jonathan, but I'm sorry it was you. She insisted I leave the bottles there after her death, but I didn't want either of you to find out this way. I was hoping you wouldn't have to find out at all."

Fuck. Bailey's world tilted, and the missing pieces of the puzzle, the ones she refused to see before, clicked together. "Was the Percocet bottle I found really full two weeks ago?"

"I shouldn't tell you this. Patient privacy and such. But she wanted you to know. I wish to God she'd told you two herself."

The words wouldn't form in Bailey's head, despite the knowledge being there. "Tell us what?"

"Four years ago, she was diagnosed with Alzheimer's. She didn't want anyone to know. The medication didn't work the way we hoped, and she was slipping."

Acid churned in Bailey's gut, and she considered telling him to stop—insisting she didn't want to hear the rest. This was a truth that needed to come out, though. "And?"

"You knew Nancy better than anyone." Dr. Phillips didn't look at her. "Knew how much her memories meant to her. She couldn't stand the thought of losing them while she was still alive."

"No."

"I tried to talk her out of it." He looked up at her with red-rimmed eyes, as if searching for forgiveness. "She made her point. Convinced me this was the right thing to do. I don't regret helping her. She went quietly, with as little pain as possible. Took her memories to the grave with her, rather than having them evaporate into nothing. Went out on a high note." Exactly what Nana used to say about Hemingway.

"*Jesus.*" Bailey couldn't hold back her sob. Nana killed herself.

"I wish there was a better way for you to find out." Dr. Phillips rested a hand on her knee. He didn't say anything else, just let her cry and handed her a box of tissues.

When she was spent, he helped her stand and let her wash her face in the sink. "Do you want me there when you tell Jonathan?" he asked.

That needed to happen. How was she going to do it? She couldn't even process it herself. "No. Thank you."

"Either one of you can call me if you need anything. Take your time in here, and leave the door open when you're done."

She nodded and struggled to keep her breakfast from repeating on her. What was she supposed to do with this information? She didn't want to deliver the news to Jonathan. But it would be best coming from her. Once she figured out how.

SIXTEEN

Jonathan braced himself for bad news when Bailey vanished for more than two hours into one of the patient rooms. Was the head injury worse than he thought?

When she emerged, he was on his feet in an instant. "Are you all right?"

She hesitated, and then gave him a weak smile. "Fine. Everything looks okay." She pretended to knock on her skull. "Right as rain, and all that."

Relief filled him. "Good." They headed toward his rental car. "Do you want to pick up lunch while we're in town? Or early dinner, I guess."

"I'd rather get back to the big house." Despite her assurance of being fine, sadness tugged down the corners of her eyes.

He held open her door for her, then hurried

around to his side. As they pulled onto the main road, he asked, "Do you want to stop at your place first? Make sure everything's intact and pick up fresh clothes?"

"Maybe later. I'm kind of tired." She fiddled with everything. Her seatbelt. Her fingers. The hem of her shirt.

"Ale?"

She didn't look up. "Hmm?"

"You sure you're okay?"

"Personally? Like physically? I'm super-duper all right. Except people keep asking me how I'm feeling. My arm's broken." She held up the sling.

He didn't like all the qualifiers. "What about not physically?"

She flopped her head against the headrest. "Once we get home." The way she clamped her mouth shut and turned her gaze out the window made him think that was that.

It didn't relieve his desire for answers.

The short drive felt as if it took forever. When they reached the house, she was out of the car before he shut off the engine. He found her in the kitchen, pacing. Out of the corner of his eye, he saw the flashing light on his phone. He had new messages, and that meant he'd had service at least for a while. It would wait. "Talk to me."

She planted her palms on the counter near the

sink and dropped her chin to her chest. "You should sit down."

"Why?"

"Because… that's what you tell people before bad news."

She'd said she was fine *physically*, and he knew they were about to part ways. What did the doctor tell her? He could stand there and second guess, or do what she asked and get answers now. "I'm sitting."

"So, I… That is—there were pill bottles in the bathroom cabinet."

"Which is good. They didn't rebel and try and take over the shower."

She turned to face him but didn't give the tiniest hint of a smile. That was a bad sign. She leaned back against the counter. "Two prescription bottles that were suspicious. Or odd. Or I'm not sure what to call them."

"Okay?" He liked this less and less the longer it went on. He was tempted to demand she spit it out, but he didn't want her to shut down.

"I—um—asked Dr. Phillips about them. Because he prescribed them. Not that he'd be able to tell me—patient doctor confidentiality and all that—but I had to ask."

"Whatever it is, you can tell me. We'll deal with it."

She dragged in a shaky breath. "Nana didn't die of natural causes."

"Tell me." His patience was vanishing beneath growing concern.

"She had Alzheimer's disease. She didn't want to lose her memories, so she…"

Fuck. He knew what came next. The reality screamed from the back of his mind. It was why Nana's letter said she'd never see him again. Why no one saw this coming. He couldn't accept it, though. A woman who loved life so much. It wasn't true. "She what?"

"Ended her own life."

Killed herself. Committed suicide. Took the selfish way out and left the rest of them behind, to cope with the consequences. A wash of black surged inside Jonathan, and he pushed back hard, swallowing it and burying it beneath a heavy blanket of numbness. "I see."

"Don't do this." Bailey frowned. "Don't pretend this doesn't matter."

It was what it was.

He didn't believe his own denial. The ink of grief rushed forward, and again he forced it aside. "You're misreading me. I'm not *doing* anything." He grabbed his phone and stood. "I need to catch up on work."

"*Jonathan,*" she called after him.

"I need to be alone." He wouldn't turn around.

Couldn't look her in the eye. Doing that would crumble the tentative wall he built inside, and he needed time to secure the barrier. Thinking about it clenched like a fist around his heart and made his step falter. He kept walking, out the front door, down the path, and God knew where beyond that.

Some place he could check into the office. A quiet spot. Checking his messages would help him focus on the people who didn't choose to give up.

Most were friends and colleagues, checking in. With each new note asking if he was all right, either because of the storm or Nana's passing, more questions bombarded him. How long was Nana planning this? Were there hints he missed? Something in her letters, about the disease and her desire to escape it? Could he have stopped it?

The thought made him clench his jaw as ambivalence rocketed through him. There was no way he could have seen this coming. Not from the woman who urged him to find his destiny. —who always had far-fetched tales to share that somehow felt real, and tied back to reality in ways he didn't understand, even now.

There were few things that confounded him, but this didn't make made no any sense. She was so full of life. Loved everything and everyone around her. Taught him to see life as an adventure. —something all too brief, to be cherished while it was here.

And it was all a fucking lie.

She didn't believe any of it. How could she spout that kind of bullshit, and then end her own existence? How *dare* she tell him—tell Bailey—he was working too hard and missing the good in life, when Nana willingly removed herself from that same life? She threw away this thing away she swore was sacred, and had the nerve before she left to say *he* didn't know how to live?

Fuck that. He reached deep inside, past the stabbing grief and bitterness and resentment, and grabbed a sheet of nothingness to wrap it all in. Work was waiting, and he'd spent a long time ensuring it went the way he wanted.

He dove back into his email inbox. It was more of the same. Meaningless condolences, wasting his time. A couple of issues in the office, accompanied by a handful of threads that ended with Liz's, *I've got this. Don't worry about it.*

That didn't take as long as he hoped.

He needed to get back to the hotel and get on his laptop. Work options were limited from here, but he could do some things. He dialed Liz.

"I'm not talking work with you," she said in lieu of a greeting.

"You have to give me something. I'm going stir crazy down here." Not quite the truth. He needed to occupy his mind. Thinking about why hit him in the gut like a fist, and he gasped.

"No. I'll talk weather. You staying dry? Is the property all right?"

Stubborn, overbearing— He cut the thought off before it became something he'd regret. Inspiration struck. "Everything's fine." The lie burned up his throat, leaving a bitter taste in its wake. "Hey. Mercy's friends with that one guy, isn't she?" Mercy was Liz's best friend and a former colleague of Jonathan's.

"Which one guy? There's a list, I'm sure."

"The one who owns Smut Central. Andrew Newton, isn't it?" Jonathan knew the answer, but he wanted to drag the conversation out.

"She is, and he does. Why?"

"We found some classic stuff here in the attic, and I'm hoping a guy with connections like his can help me put a value on it." A voice screamed in the back of Jonathan's head for him to stop, but he gagged it. The rules were different than he realized, and that meant he needed to approach this in a familiar way. Sentiment was no longer a factor. If Nana didn't believe any of the bullshit she taught him, there was no reason for him to. He could go back to living for his work without any pesky guilt. "If I ask you, pretty please, would you have her have him call me?"

"That was convoluted. Why don't you ask her yourself?"

Because making another call would give him

time to think about what he was doing. "I don't know how long I'll have service. It's spotty. I'll owe you."

"You don't owe me for passing along a message." She laughed. "I'll do what I can, but no promises."

"Thanks. You're the best."

"I know I am. Talk to you when you get back."

He disconnected and pocketed his phone. So much for distracting himself. Now this was done, his mind had a chance to wander. Except he wouldn't let it. He'd count his footsteps if he had to. Let his legs carry him to the far end of the island and back. Process quadratic equations. Repeat poetry—

Nope, not going down that road.

He lost track of time and location as he walked. When he realized he was squinting because the afternoon sun shone along the horizon and reflected off the water, he paused. Where was he? He looked around at the seaweed, the palm trees, the sand, and the battered old shack at the end of the beach. The location looked familiar, but he couldn't place it. He'd never been here before.

He traced through his mind along different points in time. Pictures. Stories. Maps. He stuck his hands in his pockets, and brushed his fingers over something metal.

He extracted the iron key. That was why this looked familiar. The trees, house, and looming cliff were in the same places as the map he'd found in the attic. The one with the key in it.

She gave her life, to keep those memories.

Which was stupid, because now they were gone anyway.

You still have them.

Great. He was talking to himself. He'd still have them even if she lived.

It wasn't your decision. Don't take this from her because you're too selfish to let her go.

"*Fuuuuck!*" He poured his rage toward the setting sun. There was no way he could hide from this. Icing over the hurt and anger wouldn't work. Fury spilled through the cracks in his defenses.

Nana was gone.

She did it on purpose.

Made the decision to leave them behind, consequences be damned.

Each new thought scraped away at his grasp on calm.

He'd have Doctor Phillips arrested. Thrown in jail to rot, for helping with such a horrendous decision. The asshole looked Jonathan in the eye and offered his condolences. *God.* Why did this hurt so fucking much?

He needed to sit down. He stumbled toward a rock near the cabin, and almost tripped on something sticking out of the sand. The corner of a box, exposed by the recent storm.

He knelt and started digging, not sure why. The wet dirt was easy to pile aside, and within moments, he dug out a space around a small wooden chest. The iron bindings on it were rusted and corroded, and the top slipped askew when he tugged it out of its hole. He wouldn't need the key after all. Even with the damage to the lock, there was no doubt in his mind the two went together.

He flipped the lid open. Water-logged foil blinked back at him in the dying sunlight. It had separated from the chocolate coins it used to encase.

A shout of frustration built inside, and he yelled into the evening, as he fell back on his ass in the wet sand. *Fucking hell.* He wanted this pain to stop.

IT WAS after eleven when Bailey heard the front door click open. She was on her feet in an instant, to meet Jonathan. It didn't matter what kind of mood he was in, as long as he was safe. She stopped short when he entered the house and stared straight at her, eyes dark and mouth pinched in pain. He was covered in sand, and half of him was wet.

She hovered a few feet back from him, unsure what to say. He obviously wasn't all right, so asking didn't make sense. "I was worried."

"I didn't realize it was so late. I'm sorry I left you

alone." Despite his haunted expression, his voice was flat.

"I'll get you a towel."

"Don't worry about it."

Now what? She searched his face, not finding answers but hoping something would come to her.

"I should have asked for a fucking autopsy. Demanded one. How naïve was I, to accept *natural causes* when there was nothing wrong with her? What Phillips did is illegal," he said.

"He prescribed painkillers to an old woman who was in pain."

"You and I both know that's not why he did it. Did he even try and deny it when you asked him?"

She hated that monotone voice. "He said she wanted us to know."

"Was she unhappy?"

"No." Bailey poured as much reassurance as she could into the reply. "Not that I ever saw. All the way up to the end, she was friendly and social and still matchmaking."

"Then why?"

"I've told you what I know. She had her reasons."

He scowled. "You sound like you agree with her."

"I don't know. I miss her. I know the loss you feel is even greater, but it still tears me apart that she's gone. This is like hearing the news all over again, but ten billion times worse. I trusted her, though. She saved my life, and I would have done the same if I could, but not if she didn't want it." Bailey's throat was raw by the time she finished talking.

"I guess you're a better person than I am. I can't forgive this." He stepped around her, and the stairs creaked with his weight.

For the second time today, she let him go.

SEVENTEEN

BAILEY COULD GO HOME NOW. THE STORM HAD passed, and while the paths would be a mess, she could pick her way through them. Sleep in her own bed. Grab a change of clothes that weren't hurriedly shoved into a duffel bag.

She didn't want to leave Jonathan alone when he was coping with this. Even if he wouldn't speak to her, she wanted to be here. She grabbed a book from the living-room shelf, and settled in to read.

The next thing she was aware of was the scent of brewing coffee. She used the smell to force her eyes open. The storm shutters were open, and the early morning sun spilled into the room, striking her face. She stretched her neck and shoulders the best she could, and her book *thunked* to the ground. Note to self—falling asleep on the couch sitting up was a bad idea. The coffee meant Jonathan was up. What kind of mood would he be in? Angry would be better than impassive. Regardless, she hoped he wouldn't shut her out.

She padded into the kitchen and found him leaning against the far counter, a mug in hand and a second sitting next to him. "For you." He nodded at the latter.

She grabbed the cup and put some distance between them again. His eyes held the same haunted look as the night before. He'd shaved. Changed. His hair was damp. Cleaning up didn't hide his grief. Once again, the words *how are you doing* died on her lips. She held up the mug. "Thanks."

"No problem." He didn't drink his coffee. Silence filled the room, and neither of them maintained eye contact. "Do you have plans this morning?" His abrupt question startled her.

"Same plans I've had all week." What she intended as teasing came out tired.

"We should go out for breakfast."

"What?"

His smile looked as though it took effort, but it was still pleasant. "We'll stop by your place, and you can change and shower. Then we'll go to *Bobbie's*. Let someone else who has food in their kitchen do the cooking. Give the locals something to talk about."

"Like what?"

"I'm not dim. Every single person we've run into since I arrived is muttering about what a cute couple we make and how it's about time. Us at breakfast together ought to make their day, regardless of the reality."

He *did* notice the stares and whispers. She shouldn't be surprised. His qualifier gnawed at something inside, but she couldn't argue. They weren't a couple; they'd both agreed. "Breakfast sounds good."

"Do you need help making sure your cast stays dry in the shower?" He winked. Like all his other expressions this morning, it looked forced.

She shook her head. "You can help me put a plastic bag around it."

Conversation was stuttered at best, as he drove them to her place. She struggled to get her clothes off around the cast without help. She needed to learn sooner rather than later. When she snagged the plaster, and jarred her shoulder, a scream tore from her throat before she could stop it. *Fuck*, that hurt.

Jonathan pounded on the bedroom door. "What happened?"

She swallowed past the jolt and let him in, relieved the spike of pain evaporated quickly. "I think I need help."

"Of course." He moved stiffly, the way he had all morning, but concern shone in his eyes. Like in the clinic, he was so gentle, working the cotton around her arm, pulling off the shirt and setting it aside, it filled her with a different type of ache. He grazed his fingers over her back. "It's a pretty shade of neon yellow now, but it's got some new purple splotches."

She smiled, but a wave of memories slammed into her from the other night slammed into her—laughing and catching up in the rain, and then sex in the shower... She stashed the images for when she was alone and not dealing with the harshness of reality. "What can I say? I'm a bruise collector." The attempt at a joke fell flat. "Thanks for the help. I've got it from here."

"I'll be in the living room." He stepped around her, gave her one final glance, and then closed the door on his way out.

After the shower, she found looser clothes. Something she could put on and take off by herself.

The diner in town was mostly empty. Even the older men who usually occupied the table in the corner were absent. The waitress was too young to know or care who Jonathan was, so there were no whispers or knowing smiles.

They ordered and still barely said more than *I'm glad it stopped raining*, and *Me too*.

Jonathan sighed. "You're dying to ask."

"I am." She hated this new information about Nana's death. Knowing didn't change anything, and she could only offer sympathy, not do the coping for him. It gnawed at her, but it seemed to be destroying him.

"Go for it."

"How are you holding up?"

"I'm not." He gave a bitter laugh. "At this very moment, I'm wondering if it'll ever not hurt. It doesn't matter what I tell myself—that I can't change the past; that this was what she wanted— I'm furious. How is it not demolishing you?"

It hurt. What she said last night was true; it was like reliving the news of Nana's passing, amplified to infinity. The pain wouldn't ebb so soon, but reason was drifting in. "Maybe it's because I was there in the end. I got to see more of her than you did. You have access to all of that, by the way. I'll tell you anything you want to know."

"Right now, I just want to know why."

"You said it yourself—this was her decision. You know her reasons."

He snarled. "But I don't understand. Do you?"

A *no* died on her lips. She tried to force the word out, but it wasn't true. "In a way, yes."

"Holy fuck." He scrubbed his face. "Do I have to put you on suicide watch?"

A wounded stab joined her grief. "I'm not considering it for myself. I respect her decisions, though. In the end, she got something few of us ever get. Control over her life and destiny."

"I can't see it that way. I hear the words, I'm trying to make sense of them, but I don't get it." He met her gaze. "And it's worse that you do. This isn't supposed to be reasonable. It was the wrong choice."

"Wrong or right, it wasn't yours to make." She hated this argument and being able to see both sides.

"I don't know if I can ever forgive her."

"I hope you do." Bailey wanted to reach for him, but he felt worlds away. "I understand if you don't. But I hope you do."

His phone rang and was in his hand before the first tone faded. Instead of answering it, he stared at the screen.

"Do you need to get that?" she asked.

"It'll wait."

For as anxious as he was to get the device back, the answer surprised her. "I'm always here to listen. Even if you want to yell about how wrong I am and she was and this all is."

"That's not me."

"I know." She covered his hand with hers. "But the offer stands from now until forever."

JONATHAN HAD to swim through sludge every time he let his thoughts drift inward. The grieving he avoided when Nana died haunted him tenfold. Heavy and sick inside. He didn't want it to go away, but he couldn't lose himself in it. As long as he only kept half his mind on what happened, he could mourn and seethe and get things done at the same time. He wanted to be mad at Bailey for brushing the entire thing off. That wasn't quite the case, though. And the agree-to-disagree approach left their friendship intact. That was important.

They got back to Nana's house—Jonathan wouldn't think of it as his. There was no doubt he'd sell the place now. Bailey settled in to her lists, and he stepped outside, to return the call he ignored earlier. He didn't need her overhearing this conversation. The number was unfamiliar, so he wasn't certain, but he had a good idea where it was from, based on area code.

"Andrew Newton." A cheerful voice picked up on the other end.

That was what he thought. "Jonathan Woodhouse, returning your call." He'd decided not to sell, but there was no reason for Bailey to know he'd considered it.

"Hey, man. It's nice to put a voice to the name. Especially for someone I've heard so much about."

"From whom?"

Andrew chuckled. "The girls and some of the guys. You know how they gossip. Get them in front of a camera, tell them to take off their clothes, and a lot of them get chatty when they're nervous."

"*The guys?*" Jonathan pulled his phone away from his ear, to glare at it.

"Teasing. Miss Mercy speaks highly of you in vague and professional terms. What can I do you for? I hear you've got antique nudies. Old Playboys maybe? Original classic pinup art?"

Jonathan wasn't sure how this guy was friends with Mercy—everything about the conversation grated on his nerves—but apparently they went way back. Kids did tend to make bad decisions. "Ernest Hemingway."

"Is that a metaphor? Some kind of *Old Man and the Sea* kind of kink?"

"It's literal. It's a film of Ernest Hemingway. But I've wasted your time. It's not for sale after all."

"Hmm." Was that seriousness in Andrew's tone? "The imagery is disturbing, but I guarantee there are buyers out there for it if you can prove authenticity. What changed your mind?"

"It's also starring my grandmother."

"Oh. Eww." Andrew sounded disgusted. "You thought about selling that? Man, what's wrong with you?"

"I wasn't in my right mind. Mourning does funny things to a person." Jonathan wondered why he returned this call. A *never mind* text would have sufficed. It was a relief to step back from the situation and view it from a different angle, though.

"I'm glad you got over it. If you come across any classic spank-sheets that don't reek of Oedipus, give me a call again."

"Oedipus was with his mother. And I didn't make the fucking movie, I found it in storage."

"Technicalities. Keep my number, but not for the incest. And I'm sorry about your loss."

"Thanks." As soon as Jonathan disconnected, rage sped back in. Was there a time limit on something like this, or was he stuck with the empty void in his chest forever?

When he wandered back into the house, Bailey looked up from her spot on the couch. "Everything all right?" She frowned. "Besides the obvious?"

Not really. Not ever again. That was melodramatic. He needed to reconcile Nana's choice or he wouldn't be able to get on with life. "I—yeah. I need to head back to my hotel and grab the rest of my things so I'm here to help you finish up, but I can't sleep in this house." His voice cracked. "Who do you like best in town, as far as lodgings are concerned?"

"Me."

"I don't think that's a good idea." Why did he say that? His subconscious didn't fill in the blanks of its assumption.

She sighed. "You're being stupid. I have a

perfectly good guest room, and my place is close." She gave him a hesitant smile. "We'll stay up late watching movies, and you can make sure I don't get into any trouble, and make breakfast."

Her teasing threatened to lighten his mood, but his resentment refused to let that happen. He covered both in numbness. "All right. But you have to behave."

"Me? I'm not the deviant."

"Whatever. I'll be your chef, but I'm not your manservant." There. That was the superficial joking he could do with anyone. The mask he was comfortable in.

"Do you want company? Driving back to your hotel, I mean. You're not the only one who's been stuck on this island for days."

He didn't want to talk, but being alone with his thoughts was worse. If she was there, they could keep up some kind of meaningless banter, and he didn't have to sink into his own head. "Sounds fantastic. We'll grab lunch and make a day out of it." He offered his hand, and pulled her to her feet when she accepted.

EIGHTEEN

BAILEY SHIFTED IN THE PASSENGER SEAT FOR THE millionth time, trying to find a comfortable position for her broken arm. It didn't hurt, but with the silence in the car, the itch under the cast became a focal point for her.

She wanted to reach out to Jonathan and comfort him, but couldn't think of anything new to say. The further they drove into the city, the more he seemed to close off. The wrinkle of a frown was gone from his brow, and his mouth was flat. No smile, no scowl, no anything.

"I didn't get to spend a lot of time exploring when I got in." Even his voice was devoid of emotion. "Where's a good place to eat?"

The break in the silence jarred and relieved her at the same time. "Depends on what you're in the mood for. Greasy? Fine dining?"

"Turkey avocado."

"You're such a California boy," she said teasingly.

His lips twitched, but no smile materialized. "They grow avocados here, too."

"But they also have fresh seafood and okra—"

"And sweet tea and grits and chicken fried steak. I'm familiar with regional cuisine, thanks. I'm homesick."

She'd call bullcrap, but she wasn't in the mood to argue. The implication he didn't consider this home—at all, apparently—dug deep. The reminder he wouldn't be here much longer hurt more. "There's a sandwich place downtown. Cali Kitchen. Ought to be perfect."

That was the end of the conversation. They reached his hotel, and rode the elevator up to his room, neither of them saying more than a few words at a time. She hovered near the door, wishing she could cross her arms.

He slid his laptop into a bag, gathered up the rest of his luggage, and shouldered the bags. A shudder ran through him, strong enough she saw his frame shake, and his things fell to the floor.

When he sank to the edge of the bed and dropped his face into his hands, her heart broke. His sob, though quiet, echoed in her eardrums like an air horn.

She crossed the room in a few strides, and knelt

on the mattress next to him. It was awkward, draping her arm around his shoulders, and pulling him into a hug, but it was her only choice. "I'm so sorry this hurts."

"She fucking lied to me. For thirty years. Fed me lines about the beauty of life. How every person should be allowed to enjoy what they had. Told me I'd be happier if I stopped every once in a while, to smell the roses. And she hated it here so much, she ran away." His interpretation of events hurt as much as the reality.

Bailey struggled with the internal war between sympathy and resentment that he didn't get this. "That's not why she did it."

"*No?*" He met her gaze with red-rimmed eyes, tears fresh on his face. "Then explain it again, because I don't fucking understand. The world is full of people who don't practice what they preach, but I thought she was a believer. She taught me our time here is sacred, and she never meant a word."

She wanted to offer sympathy, but didn't think it was the way to get through this. "You don't actually think that's true. You might hate the choice, you might loathe that she left you alone when she moved on, but you're not stupid. Part of you gets this."

"But I don't want to. I don't know how to cope with knowledge like this. The world is supposed to make sense at its core. Be ordered and logical and not driven by things like *not wanting to lose one's self.*" Anguish filled his voice.

"No one left us an instruction manual. We'll figure it out together. You have to stop trying to block up how you feel, though." Putting the thought into words hit her hard. She hadn't been able to vocalize it before now, but this was why he'd set her on edge since he arrived. No, longer—since she got engaged to Danny. It wasn't that he didn't care; it was that he refused to admit it.

"I can't. That would shred me from the inside."

She nudged him upright, and shifted them both until she could wrap his arms around her. She leaned against his chest. "So what? I disassembled me when I left Danny. I came out the other side okay."

"You had Nana's help."

"I did. And you and I have each other. Even when you go back home, we don't have to lose that." Saying the words made his leaving a more painful reality.

"Don't we?"

She pulled his arms more tightly around her. "Of course not. I'm always and forever here for you."

"I can't forgive her for leaving this way."

"I hated you for more than a decade, for letting me marry Danny, and that wasn't your fault." Bailey tried to keep her tone light, but her voice cracked.

"You're entitled to this, as long as you deal with it instead of ignoring it."

He squeezed her, and rested his chin on her head. "Thank you."

In the four days since the storm moved north, the people in town finished cleaning up debris and were well on their way to fixing up broken buildings. Bailey and Jonathan had made solid headway on going through Nana's stuff in the same amount of time. He still felt a stabbing sadness when he looked at so many of her belongings, but he accepted the grief for what it was.

Bailey was going stir-crazy, not being able to do more. She'd stayed in the living room the first couple of days, making her lists. That shifted to the occasional shout upstairs, asking what else she could do to help. Today she was wandering into Nana's bedroom every half hour or so, trying to move lighter things around. By the time lunch rolled around, he gave up trying to shoo her out.

Now they sat on Bailey's couch, her feet in his lap, *Spice Girls* playing on the TV. She told him it was his movie, so he needed to give it some love. The excuse that he was a misguided youth when he bought it didn't earn him a reprieve.

She stretched, and then settled in again. This

was his favorite position. Intimate, but without expectation. Friendly with none of that *with benefits* stuff. The way things should be.

"I'm going to miss having you as my personal slave," she said.

"I'm pretty sure that's not my title." It took him a few days to get back to being comfortable with the teasing. On some levels, it still felt wrong to enjoy life with Nana gone.

Bailey laughed. "We both know you're my bitch, as long as this"—she held up her broken arm—"has you believing I'm some sort of china doll."

"Okay, so that's true." Diving into concern for her was easier than letting the raw grief consume him. Not that he could stop the mourning all the time. When it hit, it was unrelenting. He saw it in Bailey, too. The way she paused in the middle of something, and took a few minutes to steady herself, before dragging the back of her hand across her cheeks and carrying on.

Lucifer seemed to be the only one of them dealing well with things. Once they moved her to Bailey's house, she slept at the foot of Jonathan's bed, woke up with him, and never failed to remind them if they let her food- or water- bowl drop below half full.

Speaking of food... "What do you want for dinner?" he asked.

"Whatever you're cooking. The only thing I

won't miss about you leaving is you feed me too well."

"Hang on. Processing what the hell that means." His laugh died in his throat, as her words sank in. His time here was running out, but they hadn't talked much about it. They'd exchanged contact information and then moved on to happier things.

Her smile turned sad. "I'm going to miss you, but not the fact you always make too much delicious food."

"I'll miss you too." He squeezed her foot. He wanted to say more, but couldn't make sense of the words spinning in his head, begging for release. "Spicy peanut chicken, then."

Two DAYS LATER, Jonathan loaded up his rental car. Most of the items he decided to keep were shipped home.

"Do you have everything?" Bailey asked.

He spun to face her. She leaned against the hood of the car, holding herself steady with her good arm.

"I think so." He gave his luggage one last glance, despite knowing it was all there. "I hate leaving you disabled."

"It's an arm. I'm not an invalid. I can ask anyone in town if I need something, and they'll deliver. Besides, what are you going to do? Stay for the next six weeks? You hate it here."

"I don't *hate* it."

"You're dying to get back to work." She winced. "Poor choice of words."

He wasn't trying to block the pain anymore. "You can't filter what you say. And I'd feel better if you went with me." That came out wrong. "So you're not alone while you heal." He handed her a business card with his personal information on the back.

She laughed and pocketed it. "Now that I have three, I'll probably be able to find at least one when I need it. I'm glad you came back."

"Me too." He wrapped her in a hug, careful not to jar her cast. "I'm going to miss you. Promise me you'll be safe."

She buried her face in his chest. "I promise I won't do anything stupid with my arm and that I won't get engaged to an abusive asshole and that I won't intentionally put myself in harm's way."

"I'll take it." He squeezed her tight, then let go and stepped back.

"Text me when you land."

If he said anything else, they'd be here all day and into tomorrow. He gave her a final smile and dropped into the car.

The house, and then the trees, and eventually the island grew smaller in the mirror, as he drove toward the mainland. For the first time he could remember, he didn't regret leaving it all behind. That was always his least favorite part of summer—going home at the end. There were too many memories, and surrounding himself with them would mar them, not make them better. But his other regret lingered. He'd never liked leaving alone, and the feeling was now stronger than ever.

NINETEEN

IT HAD BEEN A WEEK SINCE JONATHAN LEFT, AND IT was taking Bailey more time to adjust than she'd expected. Each time there was a knock on the door, or someone in town called her name, a tiny bit of her hoped it was him. It wasn't. Thinking such a thing was ridiculous, but that didn't stop her from clinging to the desire. They were keeping in touch, as promised. That was something.

She settled into the recliner at home with a fresh bag of chips and a jar of dip, and turned on the TV. Some sort of police procedural played in the background, as she typed out a text. *Auction's over. A few pleasant surprises. Most of it as expected. Check's in the mail.*

His reply buzzed in within moments. *If you were anyone else, I'd take that as seriously as 'trust me.'*

Or 'only driven once,' she sent back.

Or 'of course he's your son and not the mailman's.'

She laughed. *You left this movie behind without instructions. What do you want me to do with it?* Broaching the topic was risky. It meant talking about Nana's life, rather than glossing over her death.

There was a several -minute pause. Was he distracted, or did she ruin the conversation? His message finally came through. *Bury it in a crate in the back yard.*

How am I supposed to respond to that?

I'm not being bitter. Can you think of a more appropriate fate for it?

She didn't agree with his assessment. *So the next person who finds it can sell it, instead of you?*

Another pause. This one longer. *You knew about that.*

I guessed. She had hoped he wouldn't confirm it. At least he hadn't gone through with it though. *I heard pieces of the conversation. You stood on the front porch while you talked to the guy.*

Maybe the next person sells it. Maybe they burn it. Maybe they keep it and enjoy it for the classic art it is. Regardless, Nana touches at least one more life even after she's gone. Makes someone else feel. And hell, it'll drive historians nuts. Did Hemingway have another child? Didn't he?

Are you going to pursue the truth yourself? If he's really your grandfather…

No. If Nana moved on to keep her memories alive through us, I prefer them the way she shared them.

A sob welled in Bailey's chest. It wasn't all grief; some of it was knowing Jonathan finally got what Nana's passing was about. Not that Bailey expected the mourning process to be over. This was a good start, though.

IT HAD BEEN ALMOST a month since Jonathan returned home from Florida. He settled back into his routine without hesitation, but it didn't feel the same as before. Today was a good-news day, though. The kind of news that was worth champagne and a little bit of hurt. It was seven at night here, so it was ten for Bailey, but she'd still be up. He ignored how empty his condo felt. It was the same amount of populated as it had been since he moved in years ago. Furnished, top of the line electronics, stainless steel kitchen, and a single occupant.

He grabbed a glass of whiskey on the rocks and settled onto the couch. He sent Bailey a text. *That real-estate agent you recommended is a genius. Closing on the house next week.* Something about the sentence sat heavy in his gut.

Are you all right?

She was supposed to say it was awesome news,

or congratulate him. What kind of question was that? *Why wouldn't I be?*

It's her house, and it's gone now.

He tried to brush off her meaning, but it stuck to his heart. *The house is still there. I just don't own it now.*

You know what I mean.

He coped in his own way. *I'm dealing all right. Have a drink with me, to celebrate?*

Of course. Her reply was followed by a photo of a glass that looked almost identical to his.

That was better. *Cheers.*

———

SIX WEEKS since Jonathan went home. Bailey told herself she wasn't counting the days because he was gone, but because the time coincided with her getting her cast off. She still had to remind herself it was okay now to scratch when the skin itched. She stood in front of the full-length mirror in her Atlanta hotel room, admiring the way her new black dress hugged her curves and ended just above the knees. Her arm looked a little odd, being paler than the rest of her, but it would be dark in the bar. No one would notice.

She grabbed her phone, snapped a picture, and sent it to Jonathan. She followed it up with, *Hitting the clubs tonight.* The texting was a nightly ritual. He offered to call, but she told him this was more fun. She held back the part about not wanting to hear his voice. She needed a little more time before they could talk without it making her homesick from her own living quarters.

Every eye in the room will be on you. His reply flushed her cheeks. *Do you have some lucky bastard in mind, or is this a play-it-by-ear thing, to see who catches your attention?*

She was trying to get back to life as it was, but had yet to find the desire for an anonymous fling. *No guys tonight. Or girls. I'm going to dance and lose myself in the music.*

Have fun.

The brief response made her frown, but not every conversation could be a lengthy discourse on the topic of the day. She typed, *Wish you were here*, then deleted it and sent him back a simple *Thanks.*

Thank you for the earbuds. Bailey's message brought a smile to Jonathan's face. He dropped his phone on the bed and switched it over to voice text. Almost two months, and she refused to talk via phone. He didn't get it, but as long as the messages kept coming, he wouldn't push the issue.

In case you want to lose yourself in the music, without going all the way to Atlanta, he said. *Not that it should stop you.* It was *his* problem that envy snaked through him every time he thought about her grinding against other men. It would pass with time.

I don't do a lot of that now. It's not the same as it used to be.

That made his smile grow, but he'd keep his response neutral. *Maybe it's time for a new hobby. By the way, thank you for forwarding the china.* The wooden crate arrived this morning, packed up tight for its journey. The dishes Nana intended him to have when he married. He was grateful Bailey didn't sell them after all.

I had a feeling you'd want it. Wait. Why are you talking to me?

He checked his reflection and straightened his bow tie. *Are you complaining?*

Never. Don't you have that charity thing tonight?

She remembered. He liked that.

Investor dinner. It's not for an hour, and I wanted to say hi before I left.

Are you dressed to the nines and looking all spiffy? she asked.

It's my tux. Same one I wear to every dinner. I suppose since they keep inviting me back, it hasn't offended anyone yet.

I want to see.

He stared at the phone, frowning, as if the expression might carry to her. *Of me in my tux?*

Yes. I've never seen you in a tux.

I don't do selfies. He was already picking up the phone. She'd talk him into it sooner or later.

Make an exception for me?

He snapped the photo and hit *Send. Better?*

A sight I wouldn't mind seeing more often, suit or not. Though you do make it look good.

Of course I do.

As he finished getting ready for dinner, he couldn't ignore the gnawing in his chest that wished she was going with him tonight, instead of thousands of miles away.

Bailey lay on her back in bed, staring at the photo on her phone. How was it she only had the one picture of Jonathan as an adult? Okay, so maybe she was acting like a giddy teenager, crushing over the hot guy in a suit, but that didn't stop her from looking at the image every few minutes.

She missed him as much now as when he left. It might be she wasn't giving herself a chance to move on, but it wasn't as though she wanted this empty pit in her gut. It was almost two in the morning, and she couldn't sleep. Would he still be rubbing shoulders there? Did investor dinners go past eleven? Probably.

Her phone buzzed in her hand, startling her, and she almost dropped the device. That it was a new note from Jonathan chased away her exhaustion. *I miss her.* His words filled Bailey with sadness.

She was tempted to make light of the subject, simply to avoid the hurt the note summoned. She couldn't bring herself to type, *Are you drunk?* Instead she said, *Me too.*

Some days I think it's starting to hurt less, and then I remember a random thing that happened. A story she told me or a birthday gift, and the grief comes back.

It'll take time. And even then, I don't think the pain ever goes away completely. Not exactly comforting words, but it was the truth.

I know.

I'm always here, though. It was the same reassurance she always offered. This time it felt like there was more to her words than she intended.

His reply read, *<3. Good night, Ale.*

What the freak was that supposed to mean? She stared at the conversation, scrolling up to the picture of him and reading though it again and again, until the words didn't make sense anymore. She itched to call him. Suddenly her reasons for not wanting to hear his voice felt silly. He was probably sleeping instead of obsessively looking for meaning that wasn't there in a muddle of digital words.

She dropped the phone on the mattress with a sigh. What was she doing?

TWENTY

Bailey was grateful digital pictures didn't wear and tear around the edges, the way physical photographs did. She'd stopped short of making the image of Jonathan her phone wallpaper, but only barely.

A week after he sent it, she admitted it wasn't enough. *Send me another picture.* She settled onto the couch for their nightly conversation.

You know what I look like. His reply came seconds later.

But I like the reminder. What are you wearing?

Nothing.

She didn't know if it was meant to be an off-the-cuff version of *nothing special.* The image his response summoned was anything but benign. Memory blended with fantasy, teasing her with thoughts of him naked and in her bathroom, pinning her to the wall. Kissing every inch of her. *That's tempting. Send me a picture.*

You wicked girl. Are you asking me for a dick pic?

So he wasn't tossing out casual answers. If she took this further, it would hurt when it was over. She missed his touch. Whether they were screwing or just wrapped up together on the couch, she longed for it. *I might be.*

Her phone chimed with a new picture. When she pulled up the shot of his nipple, she laughed out loud. The note that followed said, *You don't get the good stuff right off.*

Still sexy, she replied.

I want one in return.

Desire raced through her, drawing her senses to life. *I didn't agree to that.*

I showed you mine…

Arousal tingled in her nipples, traveled to her belly, and focused in her core. She grasped her courage, stripped off her shirt, and snapped a picture of her bare breasts.

Wow. I got the better end of the deal.

Like what you see? Sending the teasing message was easier than giving attention to the need throbbing between her thighs.

I'll put it like this. It's a good thing I'm not wearing anything, because I'm rock hard, and slowly stroking my dick.

At the blunt confession, her skin heated to scorching. *Over a picture of me?*

Over every single picture you send me with you in it. And remembering what it feels like when you ride me.

What was she supposed to say to that?

What are you wearing? he asked.

Clothes. Wrong answer. She was so flustered, seduction eluded her.

Take them off.

She did as ordered. Though she was in her own living room, she felt exposed. Humidity kissed her skin, and dampness grew between her legs. *Now what?*

Play with your nipples.

This was a dangerous path to go down. Filled with longing that could never completely be sated. She'd care about that later. *All right,* she said.

Good. Are you moaning?

She ignored the part of her insisting it was silly to make noises with no one to hear. She wanted to enjoy this, damn it. *Yes.*

I wish I could hear you. I'm stroking my cock, thinking about you. About laying you on the bed. Kissing down your chest. Dragging my tongue up your slit, and sucking your clit until you scream.

She followed the path of his description with her fingers. It wasn't easy to text with one hand, but it was better than hearing text-to-speech repeat his messages in a monotone. *I'm playing with myself. Imagining you here, doing it for me.*

God, I love the sound of that. Finger yourself faster. I want you to come while you're thinking about me.

She could do that. She let the phone fall away, while she lost herself in the sensations. Her mind superimposed his touch over hers, drawing her into the fantasy of him buried between her legs. Licking her as she squirmed. Jerking his own shaft while he brought her to orgasm.

She whimpered and arched her back as she peaked, fingering her clit until she couldn't take the touch anymore.

You still there? he asked when she checked the screen again.

It was a good thing she didn't have to talk. She struggled to catch her breath. *Yes. I don't know if getting myself off has ever been that intense before.*

I know the feeling. God, Ale. Even imagining *fucking you makes me come hard.*

I miss you. The moment she hit *Send* she questioned the message. She'd taken things from teasing-sexy-playful to... she didn't know what.

I'm right here.

She smiled at the simple pretense. *On the other side of the country. I can't even hear you groan when you jerk off.*

Her phone rang, startling her, and she hit *Answer* without stopping to think.

"Better?" Jonathan's voice filled her head and washed over her.

She'd been wrong not to let him call before now. She needed this. "Much better."

For half an irrational second, Jonathan worried Bailey wouldn't pick up. He craved the sound of her voice. "It's still not the same." He wanted the in-person contact more, but hearing her was eons beyond reading words on a screen.

"No." Her light chuckle soothed him. "But it's a reasonable substitute."

"You could have come back with me." He knew better than to say that, but it had nagged him since he left Florida, and he was tired of holding back.

"You know I couldn't have."

"I do." He had a life here; she had one there. "I respect that. There are so many nights I wish I was there with you, watching movies again."

"You mean falling apart, while we dealt with what happened with Nana?"

He hadn't stopped dealing. Even the name dug a hole inside. "Maybe not that part."

"I miss it too, but there's nothing to do for it."

He didn't mean to take the conversation down such a somber path. "Next time, you show me yours first, then you get a dick pic."

"Jonathan." Her voice held a tone he didn't recognize.

Best to tread carefully. "Hmm?"

"If we make *this* a habit—the sexting I mean—I can't keep pretending we're *just friends*."

The phrase echoed in his head with insincerity. Not because of the way she said it, but he didn't buy it. "Is that what we're doing? I'm pretty sure neither of us believes that." He did, at first. When he got back to L.A., he told himself friendship with Bailey was enough. He still got to enjoy her company, and they weren't pulling any punches when they talked.

They *were*, though. He couldn't pinpoint when it happened, but somewhere over the last two months, he figured out he wanted more. More of her. Of them.

"What do you call it, then?" Bailey asked.

Jonathan sighed. "I didn't think I'd get a second chance at this, and I'm not going to let it get away this time. I want us to be a couple, and I'm hoping you feel the same."

"As in, boyfriend and girlfriend? Long distance lovers? Exclusive?" A happy note slid into her words.

"As in."

"So I have to stop kissing other guys when I go to the clubs?"

He knew she was joking, but he couldn't ignore the jealousy that rose inside. "I'd prefer it."

"There haven't been any other guys since before you were here."

"I know. But I still like the assurance."

She laughed. God, he'd missed that sound. "I'd love to be able to call us an *us*," she said. "Not just for the dick pics, either."

"I adore you." He grinned like an idiot in his empty condo. It felt amazing. "Does this mean you'll lift the restriction on us calling each other?"

"I don't know… I don't want you to get too spoiled."

"I already am when I talk to you." Not quite poetic, but he was more of a numbers guy.

"That's cheesy. But sweet. Call me tomorrow night?"

"I'm looking forward to it." More than he had been with anything since he got home. "Night, Ale."

"TELL ME MORE ABOUT THE PROPERTY," Jonathan said. They were in his office, talking through a proposal he'd looked over.

Aaron was one of their investment partners. Jonathan liked the guy. It was one of the nice things about building the firm the way they did—everyone got along and tended to have similar values and goals. It wouldn't work otherwise. Aaron had a quirk Jonathan couldn't seem to correct, though. The guy had a terrible eye for investments. Or rather, he wanted to help everyone, and while he picked projects that looked good on paper, he didn't have an instinct for those that would run into endless trouble.

One of Aaron's latest left him with a piece of property in downtown L.A. that he'd rather offload now, to recoup his losses, than have to manage. He was trying to convince Jonathan to take it off his hands. "Huge open floor downstairs. Seventy percent of upstairs is rented. Long-term business tenants. You shouldn't have any trouble filling the rest."

"What's been downstairs?"

Aaron cringed. "It was a gym for one of the companies that's gone now. Lots of open space."

"Coffee shop? Café?"

"Not without a lot of cost. There's plumbing in back for showers, but it all runs along the back of the building."

Jonathan wasn't in the market to rent a build-to-suit property. "You'll make more keeping it."

"I need the cash now. Red's got this idea…" Aaron's younger sister was supposedly some kind of social-engineering genius. Jonathan only knew the basic details, but she was good enough to make Aaron worth billions. The two were eternally trying to recreate the phenomenon.

Jonathan couldn't turn the property down for the price Aaron wanted. Even if the bottom floor stayed empty, and the rest dropped to fifty percent occupancy, it would pay for itself within the year. In addition, it was in a growing part of town. Jonathan was banking on urban life picking up there, and he wasn't wrong about these things. He also couldn't leave a partner stranded. "Seventy-five percent. I manage it, you get the cash, but you keep a share."

His phone buzzed, and he couldn't help glancing at the note from Bailey.

I'm heading to L.A. for a week. You're going to show me the time of my life.

Jonathan smiled and set his phone aside.

"Do you need to be somewhere else?" Aaron asked.

Jonathan shook his head. A new idea was forming, but he needed time to think it through. "Get me the contracts, and we'll go from there."

"Done." Aaron stood and shook his hand. "Thanks, man."

"No worries." Jonathan was distracted by ideas of what he'd do with that bottom floor. He hoped it worked.

TWENTY-ONE

Bailey fell into step with the disembarking crowd and made her way through the landing gate and toward the shuttles. Most of her life she'd heard that Atlanta was a miniature Los Angeles. That the West Coast city did everything bigger, better, and more Hollywood.

LAX airport was huge, but nothing compared to Hartsfield-Jackson International. It didn't matter that there were fewer people here; the crowds and distance to baggage claim were still too much. Her pulse raced with excitement, and the minutes couldn't go fast enough. She had to force herself to keep from sprinting to the carousels when she disembarked from the shuttle. Getting there sooner meant waiting longer if Jonathan hadn't arrived yet.

His memory filled her with an unfamiliar but giddy excitement. Maybe she should have talked this through with him first. Given him a hint of what she was thinking, before she made the flight arrangements. He hadn't objected to her announcement she was visiting, though, and she wanted to do this in person. Needed to discover what it would take, to see him more often.

She kept more of her attention on the crowds than on the conveyor belt, but no recognizable face stood out. She needed to calm down. If he was held up, she'd make herself sick with anticipation and then crash before he got here.

Two hands rested on her hips. Her body reacted, energy jolting through her before her brain put words to what it meant.

"I missed you." Jonathan's breath caressed her ear.

She grinned and whirled, careful not to displace his grip. Before she could answer, he tangled his fingers in her hair and crushed his mouth to hers. The kiss stole her breath and erased her doubt. She dug her fingers into his chest, needing something to hold on to, so she'd stay grounded in the middle of this amazing dream come to life.

When he finally broke away, it was to rest his forehead on hers. "I'm so glad you're here." His voice was low and gravelly.

"So am I." She relaxed and sagged into him. They'd need to have that conversation about spending more in-person time together that she'd been replaying in her head, but now she was pretty sure they were on the same page.

He snagged her baggage as it rotated past, then wrapped an arm around her waist and pointed her toward the exit. "I took the week off for this. And I promise no work while you're here, as long as we make one last stop before I sign off completely.

She tucked aside her disappointment. "What has to be done at six on a Friday night?"

"Something super important, or else I wouldn't ask. How was your flight?"

They chatted about turbulence and the sassy flight attendant and which airlines had the best snacks, as they strolled toward the parking garage. The black Mercedes sedan he loaded her luggage in was classy without being obnoxious.

"Love the car," she said.

"It gets me around." He held open the door for her, until she was seated comfortably, then made his way to the driver's side. He pulled into exiting airport traffic and inched his way along with the rest of the cars. When they made their way to the freeway, their speed lessened more. Bailey was fine with that. The thought was sappy, but she didn't mind rush hour with his company.

"Don't think I didn't notice you changed the subject," she said.

"Don't what-the-what-now?" He glanced at her.

"Hang on… Processing the double negative. No, I didn't."

"Then what kind of work needs your attention *right now*?" She wasn't trying to nag. His evasion had her curious.

"The worky kind of work." He'd never had a problem talking about his job before.

"You're acting really suspicious."

"You're reading too mu—" He snapped his jaw shut. "I might be. Short version is I took over a property that a business partner needed to dump. Got it for a good cost, and I need to see it before the weekend starts."

"Oh." That didn't sound nearly as interesting as she hoped.

He squeezed her knee. "How's Lucifer?"

"Still misses you, and doesn't like being left with a neighbor when I'm out of town."

"Then, um… give her my love?" He didn't believe the cat cared who was there, as long as someone fed her. Bailey was certain there was more to it than that. It took weeks for Luci to come out from hiding under Bailey's dresser, and she only slept on a T-shirt Jonathan left behind. Lucky cat.

The conversation shifted from one topic to the next, all of it generic. She struggled to segue into talking about how to see each other more often, but every approach she came up with felt flat in her head. Almost an hour later, he parallel parked in front of an office building that was about twenty-stories tall and made of concrete, glass, and steel.

He unlocked the front door and let them inside. The main floor spanned out in front of her, pristine white and open, only broken up by the occasional matching partition. "I wanted this to be a surprise." He grasped her wrist, raised her hand, and pressed the keys into it. "If you want it, it's yours."

"I—" She worked her jaw up and down, as her brain refused to process the obvious. "For what?"

"I was thinking art gallery." He intertwined his fingers with hers, locking the keys between them. "You don't have to. It's just a thought."

The gesture tugged at her heart and kick-started her brain with possibilities. And reality. "You remember I live about as far away from here as is possible."

"I think I got ahead of myself. Forget everything I said, but don't. Remember it, because it won't be a surprise the second time around." He tugged her toward the back of the room, around half-walls and across marble floor.

The place was gorgeous. Despite the holes in logic, in her head she was already arranging artwork.

A series of table-height shelves spanned the back wall. Strawberries and an ice bucket with a bottle of champagne sat on one. She raised her brows and turned to Jonathan. Could he hear her heart hammering against her ribs?

"I can't do this long-distance relationship anymore." He grasped her hands. "It's driving me nuts, waking up and seeing a message with your name, rather than you by my side. Hearing your voice is better, but it's no substitute for being with you. I love you, Bailey. I know Florida is home for you. That you've been there all your life, and that's where your livelihood is. I don't care where we end up, as long as…" He shook his head.

The confession of love made her heart soar, but when he dropped to one knee and looked up at her, her stomach fell into her shoes. He wasn't done. "I can work from home, as well as from the office. If you want to stay here, we'll stay. If you want me there, I'll go. This sounded more poetic in my head. Marry me?"

A giggle escaped her, and *yes* screamed in her skull. She pulled him to his feet, so she could look him in the eye more easily. "There's not much left for me in Florida. My house is a pathetic imitation of an apology from the divorce. My parents moved years ago. Nana is gone." She swallowed. "The person I love more than anything is already established here."

"So that's a…?"

She didn't know if she was dragging this out

because of hesitation or a twisted sense of sadism. "You're going to have to learn to live with Lucifer."

"I won't make you give up your cat." He twisted his mouth in amusement.

"*Your* cat. She claimed you the moment she saw you. I'll be lucky if she shares."

He drummed his fingers on his leg. "Ale?"

"You don't have hurricanes in L.A. That must be nice." There was definitely more sadism in her motivation. It was fun watching him squirm.

"We have earthquakes. You realize you're killing me about now, don't you?"

That was her cue to relent. "I'm aware. It's like I told you the night of my accident. If you asked me again, I wouldn't say *no*. I don't want to turn you down. I need you. I love you." She liked the way the words tasted, rolling off her tongue. "So, yes. I'll marry you. And yes—I want to make this into a gallery. And yes—I'm happy to move out here if it means living with you." She draped her arms around his neck and pressed close, memorizing every inch of the way their bodies fit together.

He dipped his head in, as if to kiss her, and then pulled back abruptly. "Wait." He reached into his pocket, not letting go of her waist with his other hand. A second later, he produced a small velvet box and withdrew a gorgeous, intricate golden ring. "It was my great grandmother's." He placed it on her finger, and it slid into place as if it were made for her. "Nana would have wanted you to have it."

"Only if you were giving it to me."

He finally kissed her again. Light pecks along her lips, mixed with playful nips. "Then it's a good thing it worked out that way."

He guided her backwards, until she bumped into the shelf, and trailed his mouth along her jaw, down her neck, and over her collarbone. He didn't smell the way he had in Florida. The scent of crisp rain and faint pine teased her now.

The intensity in his attention stole her thoughts. "There's a huge open window on the side of the room," she managed between gasps.

"There's plenty of cover between here and there. And would you be offended if someone tried to sneak a peek?" He sucked on the sensitive spot where her neck met her shoulder, sending whispers of pain sparking over her skin.

She simply wanted this moment with Jonathan. Anticipation slid through her, making her pulse race and her nipples tighten. "More power to them."

"Every single photo you sent me"—he drew his tongue along the edge of her ear, voice soft—"made me want you here, so I could strip you out of what you were wearing." He pulled her shirt over her head.

"Funny. I just kind of stared at that picture of

you in a tux." She leaned back, using one arm on the shelf for balance when he kissed along the edge of her bra strap and down to the cup.

He slid his finger under the fabric, caressing her skin but not exposing anything. With each new tease and touch, her head grew lighter. She dug her fingers into his arm, needing something to hold onto.

"*Just stared?* No fantasies? No temptation." He glided under the elastic to her back, unhooked her bra, and dragged her straps down her arms. When he looked her over, the heat in his gaze dialed her arousal up another notch.

"A guy who knows how to wear a suit is sexy."

"Hmm." He lowered his head to her nipple. When his tongue flicked out, she gasped. "Doesn't take much." He talked between sucks and nibbles. "Pants go on one leg at a time." He moved a hand to her other breast. Massaged and pinched. "It helps if you line up the buttons when you put the shirt on." His five-o-clock shadow scuffed her skin, driving up her desire.

She wanted more contact. More skin. She found the sense and coordination to loosen his tie. "Is it as easy to take off?"

"Easier. The buttons don't have to line up."

She fumbled her way through said buttons, losing her focus every time he scraped his teeth over her nipple. She shoved the shirt off his shoulders, and he broke away to tug his undershirt over his head before he resumed sucking.

"Better." She traced his chest with her fingers, over the flat planes, down his stomach, and along the top of his slacks.

He pressed into her, erection digging into her hip. She dipped her hand lower until she reached his shaft—a hard, eager outline. When she cupped his length and then stroked, he bucked against her touch and groaned into her skin. The vibrations trembled through her breast. Dampness pooled between her legs, and she squeezed her thighs together. Could she get off from this kind of attention? If she were more patient, possibly.

She pulled his head up and kissed him hard, memorizing the crush of his mouth against hers. There were so many sensations tucked inside this, she needed to sear every one of them into her memories. "I want you inside me."

His laugh was shaky. "I won't last long if we do that."

"That makes two of us." She unzipped his slacks. She brushed his cock with her fingers, and he jerked into her touch. The heat and temptation drove her wild with impatience.

He yanked her jeans hard enough she was surprised the button didn't pop and teeth didn't fly from the zipper, and then shoved her pants to the ground. He kissed along her thighs and stomach as he traveled back up. Grasping her hips, he lifted her onto the table behind her. "You were warned." He growled against her skin and dug his fingers in.

TWENTY-TWO

Jonathan had no restraint left. The last two months away from Bailey taxed him more than he thought possible, but now she was here. Everything about the moment was right. Her *yes* to the proposal, her gorgeous, naked body... *Her.*

He forced himself between her legs and drove into her with a single thrust. When he pounded inside, he almost came. He wanted to take this slowly. Build up to an explosive climax. She wrapped her legs around his waist and increased the pace, and he knew that wasn't happening.

Still gripping her hip with one hand, he moved the other back to her breast. When he pinched the nipple and rolled it between his fingers, her cry drilled deep into his thoughts. He knew that sound, though he'd only heard it a few times. The indicator she was close to orgasm. One of those delicious noises that teased him while he slept.

He tweaked and pounded, hammering deeper each time. Or, it felt like it. She clenched around him, groaning and embedding her nails in his back as she climaxed.

He couldn't hold back anymore. This felt too good. Tight. Slick. Perfect. Every time her pussy clenched around his cock, a surge built inside him, begging for release. He gave up trying to draw out the moment, and spilled inside her. It wasn't enough. He kept moving in and out until his body protested the pace.

As the frantic moment eased back and then they stopped, she settled her head against his chest, and he rested his forehead against her. For several moments, the only sound in the room was of them trying to catch their breath.

"We forgot the protection." Her words were muffled.

Oops. The news didn't bother him the way it should. "Is that a problem?"

"Depends on how you feel about kids."

Neutral? "I never really thought about it. I kind of like the idea."

"We've got time. I'm on the pill. But it's one of those things we have to figure out."

"And we will." He kissed the top of her head,

then placed a finger under her chin, to raise her gaze to his. "As long as we do it together."

The air conditioner kicked on, and the vent directly above them blew out a gust of chilled air. She shivered. "Maybe we should get dressed."

"I guess that was the problem with having sex here instead of home." He grabbed his shirt and draped it over her shoulders. "I'm not ready to let go of you yet."

She laughed—one of his favorite sounds—and nodded at the champagne and strawberries. "Did we miss a step in your plan?"

"Having them here sounded romantic in my head, but you were more delicious." He claimed her mouth again, loving the way she yielded and pushed back at the same time. "We should get back to my place, though."

"Oh?"

"I promised you a good time, and if I do tonight right, you won't be able to walk by tomorrow morning."

"That's a big promise. You're so arrogant some times."

"I'm up for it." He followed her gaze down. "Or I will be, by the time we get home."

She hopped from the table, and he helped her steady herself. Watching her dress, the way she moved, the tiny smiles she gave him each time she looked up—it was perfect. This felt more right than anything had in a long time. Maybe ending up with her was fate, and maybe not. But it felt as though, between the two of them, they were finally in control of their future. He liked that.

Two months later

Bailey scanned the glass coolers, trying to decide what drinks she wanted for the next leg of their road trip. The gas station sat on the edge of the California-Nevada border, and she and Jonathan were headed east. Cool air soothed her skin when she opened the door and grabbed a bottle of soda. It amazed her how warm it was for November. It would be back in Florida, too, but this was dry and she was parched.

Jonathan circled her waist from behind. She'd recognize his intoxicating scent anywhere. He traced his nose along her neck. "You almost ready, Mrs. Woodhouse?"

"That's not my name yet." She liked the way it sounded, though. Especially when he said it.

"Have you thought any more about details?"

"I don't want Elvis there, but I can't make up my mind about the drive-through." They'd decided to elope—drive to Las Vegas for the weekend and get married. She had a big fancy wedding the first time around, and it didn't help the way that relationship ended up. She and Jonathan would hold a reception later, for friends and family, but they agreed they wanted this moment for themselves.

"If you can't make up your mind, we'll go into the chapel."

"Why?" she asked.

He pointed her toward the register. "It's symbolic of our devotion and transitioning to a new life and…" He grinned when she raised her brows. "Really, I just like watching you walk."

She leaned into him. "Sounds like a valid reason to me, Mr. Woodhouse." She frowned. "It doesn't have the same ring to it."

"Still sounds like you're talking about my dad." He paid for their drinks, and they headed out to the car.

She spun to face him when they reached the Mercedes. "That's no good, then. How about Mr. Lovey-Schmoopy-Cuddly-Bear?"

He furrowed his brow, and then lunged for her and tickled her sides until she squealed. He dipped his head for a kiss. "I don't care what you call me, as long as you're the one saying it."

"That's cheesier than Mr. Lovey-Schmoopy-Cuddly-Bear. Dork."

"It's not. And I'll ask anyone in this gas station to prove you wrong." He turned away.

She grabbed his wrist. "See if the urge is still there next stop. We need to get back on the road."

"I guess." Despite the disappointed tone, he grinned.

This beat any daydreams she had of this moment, growing up. Screw the overpriced dress she'd only wear once, and the false congratulations from people who showed up because it was expected. If she'd guessed a million times how her future with Jonathan would be, she would have been wrong with each and every one. This was far better than anything she'd come up with.

THANK YOU FOR MOURNING, laughing, and celebrating with Jonathan and Bailey

If you're squirming to see what kind of woman can tame Andrew, grab RESTRAINT. Susan is his best friend's little sister, and a virgin. Andrew *really* shouldn't be fantasizing about unwrapping her under the Christmas Tree.

- Grab your copy of RESTRAINT today